Kept

LAWRENCE BLOCK
writing as Sheldon Lord

A LAWRENCE BLOCK PRODUCTION

CLASSIC EROTICA

This is for
DAVID and ELLEN

CLASSIC EROTICA #14

KEPT

Lawrence Block

Chapter 1

There's a law against hitchhiking on the New York State Thruway.

Which makes things difficult.

But not impossible. Because, while all the bulls from Buffalo to New York conspire to pull in anybody waving a thumb on the Thruway itself, none of the bulls bother you when you're standing on one of the approaches to the thing. So instead of thumbing on the road itself you wait outside on the ramp and catch the cars on the way in.

It's very easy to stop on the ramp. It's easy to see the smile and the pearly white teeth and the valiant and hopeful thumb, so I smiled and showed the pearly teeth on the goddamn ramp leading into the Thruway, as I guess you may have figured out by now, and it was Entrance Twenty-two just south of Albany. I was southbound, headed for New York.

I had been standing in the same silly spot for almost half an hour. Half an hour isn't an especially long time to wait for anything, from a ride to a girl that you're taking out dancing, but when you're hitching it *seems* longer. I was beginning to get the feeling that I wasn't making any progress whatsoever, which was quite true, and that I might very easily stand where I was for the rest of my life. Hitching is a tenuous thing, tricky as a warped cue, and you can never be sure quite where you are.

Cars kept passing me. It was close to three in the afternoon and the sun was burning monotonously into the back of my neck. I had a pretty good tan from the three weeks I had spent on a road crew but I was still feeling the sun and I had a strong hunch I'd be feeling it for days. The white cotton laundry bag slung over my shoulder held everything I owned in the world, which was very little. But half an hour in one spot with the sun on your neck greatly increases the weight of anything, even a little white cotton laundry bag. I wanted to drop into a shaded pit of ice water and think cool thoughts.

A grey Mercury slowed down while the driver took a long look at me. I guess he didn't like me—he looked away and speeded up and that was the end of him. I didn't much like me, either, and I could sympathize with the son of a bitch. I needed a shave and there were circles under my eyes. I didn't have to see the circles. I could feel them. They felt heavy.

Another car passed. And then another car passed. And another and another and another, and did you ever stand by the side of the road on a hot day in August and watch the cars go by? For awhile you count them, and then that gets boring and you switch to just counting the convertibles, or just counting the *red* convertibles, or something shrewd like that.

You do this because you think it'll help pass the time.

It doesn't.

But you keep going, counting and tapping your foot and maybe humming songs to yourself, smiling like a choirboy and thumbing with a passion.

And, some time or other, a car stops for you.

A car stopped for me.

It was a brand new Cadillac convertible. And a convertible is definitely not the type of car that picks up hitchhikers. This one was fire-engine red, which means I would have counted it if I had been counting red convertibles at the time.

I told you about the type of car that picks up hitchhikers. There is also a type of driver. The type is between 45 and 60 and he is so friendly you could give up friendship for life. He either chain-smokes cigars or else doesn't smoke anything and minds if you do.

This driver was not the type.

This driver was a woman. Not a woman who looked like she could be the wife of the guy described above. Not by any stretch of the imagination.

She was a woman who went with a Caddy convertible, long and sleek and smelling of money. She had blonde hair that was too perfect to be phony and she had the brains to wear it shoulder-length so that there was more of it. That was the way to do it. It was the type of hair there should be more of, the more the merrier.

She was wearing one of these off-the-shoulder dresses that

always wind up off-the-breasts, and there was a lot of her to look at. It was worth looking at, full and high and obviously all hers.

By the time she managed to ask me where I was headed I already had my laundry bag in the back seat and my tail planted on the front seat a respectable distance from hers. I told her New York and she gave me a quick smile and told me that she was driving all the way to the city. I was in luck; it wasn't going to be one of those short hauls that doesn't do much more than break the monotony of standing in one place. But I didn't even think about it. If she had been driving to Bombay I probably would have gone with her. She was that type of doll.

She got the car going again and drove the rest of the way on the ramp, took a ticket from the clod at the entrance way and drove out onto the Thruway. She didn't say anything at first, just concentrating on her driving and giving the big Caddy its head. A minute later she was doing eighty and it felt like fifty.

It was a pleasure to watch her drive. Most women drive the way I speak Spanish. I had two years of it back in high school and I can still make myself understood, but it's not my language. That's the way it is with a dame behind the wheel. She may not do anything wrong, but she never gets the feel of the machine or the feel of the road or any kind of a feel outside of the one the guy next to her is giving her. To hell with the insurance statistics—women are lousy drivers. They're nice to look at and fun to make conversation with and pure heaven to bang, but they should never—repeat never—be allowed behind the wheel of an automobile.

With the exception of this one. She handled the car flawlessly and you could see that it wasn't the usual battle between woman and machine but a game she and the Caddy were playing. She understood the car, and she knew what it could do and was pretty damned proud of it. And the car knew who was driving it and knew the driver was good. She cut out to pass a fat little Ford that was meandering from lane to lane like a drunken beetle, slipping around the Ford and winding up in front of it with one motion, one perfect and almost beautiful S-curve.

We didn't talk at first. She drove and kept her eyes on the road while I sat and thought and kept my eyes on her. I had the better end of the deal; she was a lot more fun to look at than the New York State Thruway, engineering marvel though it may well be. I'd just finished getting fired from a road crew, and I knew a little about construction, and I was all in favor of hers.

Her legs were long and slim, and the dress wasn't long enough to keep me from seeing the trim ankles and the neatly rounded calves. The rest I had to guess at, but with a dress like that guess-work is easy and with a body like that it's a pleasure. Swelling thighs. Hips that were made for horizontal business. A flat stomach and a slender waist. Arms and shoulders tanned a golden brown like a field of summer wheat ripening under a hot sun.

She drove and I looked at her, and half the time I thought about her. That got painful after awhile, so the rest of the time was devoted to thinking about the job in Albany. Not a bad job, if you like to work ten hours a day at a job that gives your brain a chance to think about other things. Road work—pick-and-shovel stuff that gets you into shape and fills up your wallet at the same time. A good sixty hours a week, and twenty of those hours at time-and-a-half for overtime, which isn't bad when the pay is upwards of three bucks an hour to begin with.

If it hadn't been for Corrigan I'd still have the job.

Corrigan was the foreman—a big dumb Mick who stood about six-three and weighed somewhere around 250. Corrigan got to be a foreman by being a good worker and a frighteningly decent sort of a guy.

And all was hunky-dory.

Until Corrigan fell in love.

A guy like Corrigan falls in love with a thump. He fell, to be precise, like a ton of wet concrete, and he fell for a silly little slut named Sally Austin. Corrigan, naturally, was firmly convinced that Sally Austin was the most wholesome thing since his mother's apple pie. This wasn't entirely true, for while Corrigan was taking her to movies and giving her a chaste kiss at her door, Sally Austin was putting out for half the male population of Albany and taking great pleasure in the happy little process.

She was a skinny little kid with clear blue eyes and a nice-if-boyish body and white teeth that flashed in a lay-me smile whenever there was a man within shooting distance. Her hips and thighs had so much muscle from bedroom games that she wouldn't have had much trouble getting a road crew job if she wanted one.

She also had very little trouble getting a job from the road crew. Corrigan never had the slightest notion, but every man who wanted action was boffing the foreman's girl whenever the foreman's back was turned. For a few weeks I ignored the flashing white teeth and the lay-me smile. Then I stopped ignoring it.

I took Sally Austin to a motel on the west side of Albany and kept those well-trained hips churning for most of the night. She was lots of fun in bed and fun to be with between sets. She had little freckles on the tip of her nose and short black hair and breasts that were small but perfectly formed, firm even when she was lying on her back, which was most of the time. A nice kid, a fun kid, a hell of a partner in bed with more tricks than a 42nd Street magic shop.

But not a particularly good prospective wife for a nice slob like Corrigan.

So I made like a nice guy, which is somewhat out of character for me and not particularly intelligent. I told Corrigan, and when he laughed like it was a joke I told him again, and when he looked at me and didn't know whether or not to believe me I told him in detail, mentioning the cute little mole on her stomach about two inches above her navel and things like that.

The first punch lifted me off the ground and carried me half-way out of the world. I had a horrible moment when I thought I was going to get killed, but Corrigan was such a nice slob that he played by Marquis of Queensbury rules. He waited for me to get up and then came at me with his fists, anxious to take my head off and play basketball with it.

Marquis of Queensbury rules are fine and jolly if you don't really care who wins. I cared, and when he threw the second punch I stepped back away from it and kicked him as hard as I could between the legs. He let out a bellow they must have heard as far west as Schenectady and held himself where it hurt.

So I hauled off and kicked him in the head.

This took care of the fight, but it also took care of my association with Miller Bros. Construction, Inc. I gave the money I had meticulously saved up to the hospital to take care of Corrigan—a kick in the groin and a kick in the head were not covered by workman's compensation. And then I got the merry hell out of Albany, which is a pretty grimy little town anyhow, and here I was in a fire-engine red Caddy convertible, sitting on a genuine leather seat next to a babe who could give Sally Austin cards, spades, and the ten of diamonds and still come out well ahead.

I wasn't complaining.

By the time we hit the Poughkeepsie cut-off the babe slowed the Caddy to a sluggish 75 and became aware that she wasn't alone in the car. She glanced at me out of the corner of her eye and sort of half-smiled at the road.

It was my cue.

"Sure appreciate you picking me up," I said. "It was getting pretty hot out there."

"This is the first time I ever picked up a hitchhiker."

"It can be dangerous," I said.

"Can it?"

"Sure. For all you know I'm an escaped rapist."

"Are you?"

"No."

She laughed. It was a good laugh, free and easy and happy. It made me wish I had said something funny enough so that I could join in and laugh along with her. She looked like she'd be loads of fun to laugh with.

"I don't know quite how to go about this," she said, not too convincingly. It was tough to believe there was much of anything she didn't know how to go about. "How do you talk to a hitch-hiker?"

"You call the shots," I told her. "When you pick someone up, it's up to you to let him know whether he should listen to you or talk to you or whether you should both just sit there and watch the scenery. It's your car, so he has to play it whatever way you want. If you ask questions he has to answer them. He can lie if he feels like it, but he has to play ball one way or the other."

"That's very nice," she said. "I should have picked up people before. It sounds entertaining."

"How do you want to be entertained?"

She thought for a minute. "Why don't you tell me about yourself?" she suggested. "Maybe that will be entertaining."

"I'm not particularly interesting."

"That doesn't matter." She flicked off the radio, which by now had given up music completely and switched to rock-and-roll, and said: "You can't be worse than that noise. But don't lie to me. Tell me the truth."

"Where should I start?"

"To begin with," she said, "who in the world *are* you?"

I gave her the quick biographical sketch, telling her the truth because it was easier than lying. I told her my name was Mark Taggert and that I was a transplanted New Yorker who hadn't managed to put down roots anywhere. Twenty-eight years old, with a ridiculous past and not much of a future. The past included a high school education and a year-and-a-half of college in New York, two unproductive years in the army, and short-term hitches at everything from pearl-diving in a Cape Cod chowder house to selling no-money-down auto insurance for a fly-by-nighter in Syracuse, with gandy dancing and ditch digging and fruit picking scattered in between, along with other jobs too monotonous and numerous to mention.

No family to speak of. Parents dead, one brother quietly rotting away in a state hospital for the incurably insane, an uncle in California whom I hadn't seen in upwards of fifteen years and who I could go another fifteen years without ever wanting to see. A few hundred buddies scattered all over the world but no close friends because I never stayed in one place long enough to form anything resembling a permanent friendship type of thing. Never married, no children that I knew about, no ties of any sort and no prospects, vocational or otherwise.

Mark Taggert. A drifter coming from no place and going nowhere, and in no particular hurry to get there. Mark Taggert, unemployed, with maybe fifty bucks in my wallet and confetti in my head. I talked slowly and easily because it was relatively easy to talk to her even if I had nothing at all important to tell her, and she took it all in from beginning to end without saying much of anything. Once in a while her face would hold the shadow of a smile; other times a slight frown would crease her forehead and her lips would turn down at the corners. But most of the time she just paid attention to her driving and it was hard to tell whether she was listening or not.

When I finished she asked me why I was going to New York.

"I don't know for sure," I said. "It's a place, as good as any of the rest and better than most of them. I'll find some kind of a job and some kind of a place to live and stay there until there's some other place that looks better. That's all."

"What will you do there?"

I shrugged. "It doesn't much matter. I've done enough different things so that I can get a job without any trouble. Nothing that pays too well but enough to live on."

She nodded. The conversation died there and we sat around waiting for it to get started by itself again.

"Now what?" she said finally. "Do we just sit and watch the scenery again or do you keep on talking?"

"Anyway you want it. You can ask me questions or you can talk or whatever."

"What would I talk about?"

"You could talk about yourself," I offered. "If you feel like it."

"Why don't you talk about me?"

"Huh?"

"Yes," she said, half to herself and half to me. "Maybe that would be nice. You see, it wouldn't entertain me to tell you about myself. But you've been sitting here for awhile and you must have formed some impression of me. Why don't you tell me about it?"

"I don't really know anything about you."

"You can guess, can't you?"

"I suppose so."

"Go ahead."

I hesitated. I've been enough places and known enough people so that I can size up a person fairly well. I notice things that most people don't notice—I have to, because I rarely know anyone long enough or well enough to get by just soaking up surface impressions. I could probably tell her more than she expected about herself, but I didn't know how much of it she would want to hear. People get visibly disturbed by a guy who notices too much.

Then I decided I didn't really give much of a damn whether she got disturbed or not. The worst that could happen was that she might tell me to get out of the car, and I seriously doubted that something like that would happen. What the hell—she was calling the shots.

"You're about twenty-six years old," I said. "You're an unusually attractive woman and you're completely aware of it. You have quite a bit of money and you're pleased because you like having money."

I took a breath and studied her face. It was expressionless and it was impossible to tell how she was taking it. What I had told her so far wasn't the work of genius—it was relatively obvious.

I kept going. "You inherited the money," I said. "Your family had money and your husband had even more money. You were married once, but if you're still married you're not working very hard at it. You might be separated or widowed, but you're probably divorced. No children.

"You live in New York now but you weren't born there. You were born either in Upper Westchester or Connecticut, but probably Westchester. Your father was a professional man rather than a businessman, and you went to a private school but one where you lived at home."

I paused.

She said: "Keep going."

"You went to college in the East," I went on. "Not Vassar or Radcliffe but something in that bracket. You weren't a virgin when you got married but you didn't cheat on your husband, or if you did you never made a habit of it. Now that he's either dead or divorced you've been to bed with somebody, but it's nothing serious. You're free now."

"What else?" Her voice was trying to be light and easy but it didn't make it.

"Nothing else," I said. "I don't really know you, you see."

"Aren't you going to tell me what I'm like in bed?"

"You're great in bed," I said. "You're a tiger."

After a long, flat silence she said: "Okay—tell me how you knew all that."

"I guessed."

"The hell you did. Nobody guesses like that."

"I made some observations and took off from there. That's all."

"Tell me how you did it."

I took out a cigarette and offered her one but she shook her head. I lit mine with a match and tossed the match out of the window. I blew out smoke and turned to look at her again.

"A lot of it was easy," I said. "You were married because there's a white band on your ring finger where there used to be a ring. If you were a widow you'd probably still be wearing it, same if you were separated. You're not going with anybody now or you wouldn't have picked me up.

"Your accent told me where you were from, that coupled with the words you use. You couldn't be from New York City or you wouldn't drive as well as you do. The bit about school was a calculated guess, like the bit about your family."

"How about my sex life?"

"Oh," I said. "Call it male intuition or something. That was a guess, too."

"You're too good a guesser."

"How close did I come?"

"Too close," she said. "You make me feel as though I'm not wearing any clothes."

"Where was I wrong?"

"Nowhere, really. My name is Elaine Rice and I'm twenty-five. Married to a rich and useless guy and divorced from him. Born in Pound Ridge, college at Wellesley. Two affairs before marriage and one abortive one since. My father was a doctor. And you're too damned clever, Mr. Taggert."

We took it from there. She talked about herself and we kicked around everything from the state of the world to why football was a better game to watch than baseball. She stopped on the road at a Savarin for coffee and a bite, and when I tried to pay the checks she wouldn't let me. Then I tried to pay my share and she wouldn't let me do that either.

We were back on the road a half hour later and still talking. By this time I wasn't thinking of her as a quick ride to New York any more. I was thinking of her as a ride, but one without the Caddy.

It was a dangerous way to think. She was everything and I was nothing, and I'm saying this without selling myself short. She was rich and beautiful and poised and bright, and I had fifty bucks in my wallet and nothing else in the world besides the junk in the laundry bag.

But try thinking of something else when you're sitting next to a woman like Elaine. Try looking at breasts like hers without wondering how much of them would fit in your hands. Try looking at those legs without wanting to . . .

Try it.

It's impossible.

We left the Thruway and wound up on the Major Deegan and finally on the East Side Drive. The East Side Drive is officially known as Franklin Delano Roosevelt Drive, in case you're interested, but it's called that even less than Sixth Avenue is called Avenue of the Americas. We left the drive in the thirties and headed west.

Not too far west. She took a left at Park Avenue and pulled the car into a driveway between 35th and 36th. A monkey in a uniform appeared and called her Miss Rice and drove her car into a garage. We were standing there and I was sort of staring at nothing when she slipped her arm into mine.

"Come on," she said.

My mind wasn't working very well. I just looked at her for a minute.

"This is where I live," she said. "You'll come up for a nightcap, won't you?"

It was a few minutes to seven and the sky was still bright and joyous. It was hardly the time for a nightcap.

I didn't argue with her.

She lived in this residential hotel where the rent is something I'd rather not talk about and where there is at least one servant who doesn't seem to do anything but polish doorknobs. We walked into the gold-plated lobby and she hung on my arm very nicely, with her dressed in this gorgeous off-the-breasts thing and me in my tee-shirt and dirty khaki pants. I still needed a shave and the circles under my eyes were heavier than ever.

Nobody even seemed to notice us, ridiculous as we must have looked. They train them well in those Park Avenue hotels. The desk clerk handed her a key as if he were delivering a message to Garcia and the elevator operator whisked us up so smoothly we didn't seem to be moving at all. At the fifteenth floor the car stopped and we got out and walked down the hallway to her apartment. The carpet in the hallway was the kind you have to mow every two weeks with a lawnmower.

She put the key in the lock and turned it and the door opened. The apartment looked like a miser's wet dream and that good old money smell was all over the place. She turned to me and gave me one of those butter-wouldn't-melt-in-my-mouth-but-there's-another-place-where-it-would looks.

"Sit down," she said. "I'll make us some drinks."

I sat down.

Heavily.

Chapter 2

The apartment is worth describing. The carpet was like the one in the hallway except more so, a rich, wine-red affair that looked too expensive to step on. The furniture had the simplicity of class, nothing the least bit ornate and nothing that didn't cost plenty. Mahogany it was, matching pieces of perfectly polished mahogany, with a little coffee table just a foot or so off the floor and a hi-fi in one corner and a massive desk on the far side of the room.

The records in the cabinet next to the hi-fi showed the same taste, or maybe I'm prejudiced because her taste happened to coincide with my own. A little New Orleans jazz—Johnny Dodds type stuff, and a lot of modern stuff running from Bird to Mingus with the emphasis on the hard bop stuff. The jazz took up about half of the cabinet and the rest was full of the type of classical stuff that more people should listen to—Bach and pre-Bach, Vivaldi and Tartini and Corelli and Scarlatti and people like that. I hauled out a Vivaldi bassoon concerto and stuck it on the turntable and pressed a button. The hi-fi had perfect tone and the recording was excellent.

I sat down again, this time on a couch that was even sleeker and softer than the chair I sat on the first time. I looked at the abstract prints on the walls and discovered that they weren't prints. They were originals.

Money.

Money and class.

She came back a minute later with two glasses. They looked like glasses of water except that there was an olive in the bottom of each, and I knew right away that this doll knew how to make martinis. The secret is all in the amount of vermouth you use. The less vermouth you slosh in, the better the martini turns out.

"Martinis," she said, which was unnecessary. She handed me mine and sat down on the couch beside me, curling those long legs underneath her. I sipped the drink and nodded appreciatively.

"Good music," she said. She moved close to me on the couch so that our bodies were only an inch or so apart. I wanted to put my arm around her but something held me back. Maybe it was the contrast between the clean richness of her and the dirty tee-shirt and khakis. Whatever it was I didn't make a move.

"You're a funny guy," she said. "I can't figure you out at all."

"There's not much there to figure."

"I'm not so sure about that. You're too damned clever. You notice too much."

"It's just a knack."

"Maybe, but it's rather highly developed with you. I think I'm a little bit afraid of you."

"Of me?"

She nodded, and I decided that she was mildly nuts. If she was afraid of me she selected an odd way to show it. When you're afraid of somebody you don't ask him up to your apartment for a drink that is a fairly obvious prelude to a trip to the bedroom.

I left it there and we talked about other things, like what a bastard her husband was. Only it turned out that he wasn't really a bastard, just a spoiled perpetual adolescent who couldn't really help himself. It was one of those wild courtship type things with dates at the Stork Club and 21 and shows and flowers and both of them acting parts without entirely realizing they were acting, until suddenly they were married to each other without entirely being aware of that either.

Then a honeymoon—Europe, Paris, the Italian Riviera, the Grand Tour, and no chance to find out that they weren't in love with each other because they were too busy going places and doing things. They still weren't married, not really. They still didn't know each other, and it was still a storybook type of scene with a handsome guy and a beautiful woman and plenty of money, going places and doing things and never knowing where in the world they were going or what in the world they were doing.

By the time they were back in the States and settled in New York they didn't know what the hell was coming off. They still went night-clubbing and partying and vacationing, but they couldn't spend a quiet evening at home because the more they got to know each other the more they realized that they didn't belong together at all. He started drinking too much to escape and she started sleeping twelve to fifteen hours a day, just as much of an escape but considerably easier on the liver. And the marriage ended by mutual consent with a quick divorce in Nevada and a fat settlement. It was never much of a marriage to begin with and they were both pretty anxious to put an end to it. They lasted a little less than a year, all told, and according to her that was a good bit too long.

I listened to all of it and nodded and clucked in the right spots, and by the time she was through the Vivaldi was also through and the needle was making the clicking sounds it makes when a record is done playing. It was about this time that we found out our martinis were finished. She smiled quickly, a smile that was warm and nervous at the same time, and then she took the empty glass from my hand and stood up.

"Flip the record while I fill these up again," she said. "There's a Corelli sonata on the other side that's kind of nice."

The Corelli was a violin sonata that was more than kind of nice, and I was sitting on the couch enjoying it when she reappeared with more martinis. I took mine and sipped it and by this time I was beginning to feel the effects of the first one. Martinis give me a very pleasant edge. I talk easier and feel better about most things, and right now I felt fine.

She sat a little closer to me this time but our bodies were still separated by a half-inch or so. And I still didn't put my arm around her.

"You scare me," she said. She was back to that again.

"How do you mean?"

"I don't know you. I don't know you at all."

"You've only known me for a few hours."

"That's not what I mean," she said. "I can't tell what you're going to do, how you're going to react. I can usually sense how a person is going to behave, but not with you. You're fairly unpredictable."

I couldn't think of anything especially unpredictable that I had done so I didn't say anything.

"You must know why I asked you up here."

It was sort of a question, but since she didn't end it with a vocal question mark I didn't feel called upon to answer it. I gave a non-committal shrug.

"I asked you up here because I wanted you to make love to me. You know that, of course."

I didn't say anything. I looked at her but I couldn't see her eyes. Her face was turned floorward and she was apparently gazing at the rug.

"You know that," she repeated. "And I'm fairly confident that you find me attractive and that you'd like to sleep with me. I've been waiting for you to make a pass at me. But you haven't, and I don't know why you haven't, and I'm not sure whether or not you're going to get around to it."

She. turned and looked at me, and the tension in her face was there for me to see. There were little lines at the corners of her mouth and tears welled up in the tear ducts of her eyes. But the tears wouldn't spill out. She wasn't going to cry; she was just very much on edge.

"I'm so unsure that I've had to say this," she went on. "Now I've forced you to make a pass, and that's not the way to go about things at all. I realize that. But . . . but I'm not sure of myself at all any more.

"Now you must think I'm a tramp," she said. "Miss Richbitch, the slut of Park Avenue."

I told her to shut up. My voice was husky and sounded weird to me.

"I don't care," she said. "I want you. That's all."

I tilted her head up toward me and kissed her. It was all she needed, tense as she was, and her arms went around me at once and our bodies were pressed together. Our mouths opened and our tongues met and became good friends at once.

We kissed again. Then I took that beautiful head in my hands and kissed her all over her face. I kissed her nose and her eyes and the tip of her chin. Then I found her lips again and kissed them and she began to breathe faster.

"Mark," she said after we came up for air. "This is so silly and so perfect. Kiss me again, Mark."

I kissed her again.

"The bedroom is through that doorway," she said, nodding toward a doorway. "If you don't take me there in a minute I'll lose all my pride."

"Then what'll you do?"

"I'll drag you there," she said. "By the hair."

"You won't have to," I said. I stood up with her in my arms and her arms around my neck. She was easy to carry and soft and warm in my arms. Her eyes were on fire.

The Corelli record played on. If I didn't change it or something it would be bad for the needle.

To hell with the needle.

• • •

The bedspread was off and the covers were turned down. She had everything all ready, which was considerate of her. I told her so.

"Don't talk," she said through clenched teeth. "Don't say a word. We can talk later."

She had the right idea. She stood up after I had set her down on the bed and came into my arms. Her whole perfect body was pressed tight against me and her arms were bands of soft steel around my back.

I didn't kiss her or stroke her. Petting has its place but this was not the place for it. Instead I lifted her in my arms and placed her on the cool white sheet. Her body was lovely against it and her hair spilled over the pillow like liquid gold. She was tanned evenly all over, with the tan just a touch lighter on her breasts and belly.

Her breasts tight against my chest, so soft and firm and pressed so close I was afraid I would hurt them. Her breath, hot as a blast furnace on my cheek. Her heart beating at top speed in time with mine.

It was fast and intense and hot as the center of Hell. It wasn't human; it was two animals in the jungle with hyenas screeching in the distance and a bed of warm jungle grass beneath our bodies. It was the world spinning at twice its normal speed, gathering us up and floating us higher and higher, pitching us past the boiling point, turning day into night and night into day and day back into night again.

Higher and higher.

My teeth sinking into her shoulder.

Her nails like tiger claws raking my back and drawing blood.

Higher and higher.

And still higher, until we were together at the top of the world with everything else at our feet.

Then higher, and everything else disappeared.

Two simultaneous claps of thunder.

Then peace, with our bodies together and naked and slippery with sweat, and a little voice in my ear saying my name over and over and making it sound like a prayer.

"Mark?"

"What is it?"

"It was wonderful, Mark." Her voice was suddenly a whisper, hushed and soft in my ear. I held her close to me and she was soft and warm and sweet-smelling.

She didn't have to tell me it was wonderful. It was the best, the most perfect, the ideal. It was something neither Thelonious Monk nor Antonio Vivaldi could ever match. Elaine was hardly the first woman I had had, hardly the first one I had taken a great deal of pleasure in making love to.

But she was the best.

"Yes," I told her. "It was wonderful."

"It was never quite like that with anybody else."

"There never was anybody else."

"You're right," she said. "You're right. They're gone, those others."

"They never existed."

She kissed me. Her lips were soft now, and a rich red even though all her lipstick had been kissed away long ago. I returned the kiss and drew away from her slightly, running a hand the length of that magnificent body. I touched her neck first and moved my hand over her breasts, over the flat stomach, down past the hips and thighs and calves.

"Do you like my body?"

"You know I do."

"Tell me anyway."

"I like your body."

"Tell me again."

"I love your body."

"Mark—"

I waited for her.

"I like your body, Mark. You're very strong, aren't you?"

"Not too strong."

"Yes, you are." She reached out a hand and wrapped it around my biceps.

"Make a muscle," she commanded.

I made a muscle.

"Mmmmm," she said. "Strong."

She wrapped her arms around me, and I didn't mind in the least.

"Then," she said, "You must be hungry."

"I am."

"Want to go get something to eat?"

"No."

"No?"

"No."

"I can fix you something right here and we won't have to go out or anything. I can make a sandwich or something. It'll only take me a minute."

"No," I said.

"I thought you were hungry."

"I am."

She said: "Oh," and her eyes were wide and sparkling.

"See?"

"I see. I told you that you were strong."

I took her in my arms and kissed her, tasting the sweetness of her mouth, feeling the sweet softness of flesh against flesh. I kissed her throat, kissed the little hollow in the base of it where her pulse was beating steadily and rapidly.

I kissed her again and she was ready for me, and I took her in my arms and we were making love again, our bodies together and our lips together and our hearts racing in time with each other.

The needle was scratching on the Corelli sonata. The record had finished long ago, and the needle was scratching away at the plain plastic in the center of the record.

Neither of us heard it.

CHAPTER 3

She wasn't a bad cook. At least she made decent scrambled eggs, and that's something. She also made good coffee, which put her way out in front of ninety percent of the restaurants in the United States.

We were sitting on opposite sides of an intimate little table in the intimate little kitchen. She was using a quilted housedress to hide the loveliness of her body and I was wearing a clean tee-shirt and a clean pair of khakis from the laundry bag. She had called room service and had them send a boy to haul the laundry bag up from the car, which was sort of silly, actually. The quarter she gave the kid was about the net value of the junk in the bag.

The Corelli sonata had long since been returned to its jacket and replaced in the cabinet, and now the Modern Jazz Quartet was playing "Django", a beautifully bluesy lament for a three-fingered guitarist named Django Reinhardt. It made good dinner music—moody and unhappy, but a nice accompaniment for scrambled eggs and black coffee. John Lewis on piano and Milt Jackson on vibes and Percy Heath on bass and Kenny Clark on drums, and it was one of their early sides before they got lost in fugue structure and college tours and their music turned into background slush for slick magazine stories.

I looked across the table at her and she was beautiful, even with her face devoid of makeup and the housedress making mole-hills out of mountains. I spooned a mouthful of egg into my face and swallowed a big glug of coffee. Then I reached for a cigarette and set it on fire, noting with approval the way a cigarette and a cup of good coffee went together like beer and pretzels. Then I looked at her again. She was a pleasure to look at.

I glanced at the clock on the wall behind her—it was pushing nine-thirty. Time to cut out if I wanted to get a hotel room for the night.

"Elaine?"

She looked up at me.

"I better get out of here pretty soon."

"What for?"

"Have to find a place to stay."

"Don't be silly."

"Well, if I don't get started soon it'll be tough to find a hotel that isn't full and—"

"What in the world do you want with a hotel?"

"Well, until I can get a decent room or apartment—"

"Mark," she cut in. I stopped and looked at her.

"Mark," she said again, "what on earth do you want with an apartment?"

"Gee, I dunno, Ma'am. Always figured it'd be good to have a roof over my head, but I reckon—"

"I have an apartment, Mark."

"I know," I said. "I've been there, Ma'am. Grown right fond of parts of it. The bedroom, in particular. Shore beats layin' around on a pallet on the floor, Ma'am."

"There's room for two here," she said softly.

Hey—"

"And I . . . want you here. With me."

I thought for a good half-second, then shook my head. "No," I said. "I can't stay here, Elaine."

"Why not?"

"The rent's too high."

She stared. "What do you mean? I wouldn't charge you anything, you idiot. What—"

"Then it's too low."

"I don't think I understand you."

"Don't you?"

She shook her head.

I took a deep drag on the cigarette and chased it with the last swallow of coffee. Then I blew out the smoke in a thin gray column. I looked at the smoke until the column broke when the air-conditioning blew it around the room. Then I took another puff of the cigarette and repeated the process and ground the butt out in a big black ashtray. While I was doing this I could feel her eyes on me, probing, trying to search my face.

"It's very simple," I said. "I pay for what I take. I can't live here because you would be paying my rent and I don't like to do things that way."

"That's what I thought you meant."

"Then why did you say you didn't understand?"

"Because I don't, Mark. I don't understand why you think that schoolboy reasoning makes any sense."

It was my turn to stare.

"You pay for what you take," she went on. "Because I have money and you don't, you think you should live in some ratty hotel and be away from me. Why?"

"Because—"

She didn't let me get the words out. "You pay for what you take. What about me? How are you paying for what you got from me in the bedroom if you won't even stay with me?"

"I'm sorry," I said. "I thought you enjoyed it."

That hurt her more than I meant it to. She lowered her eyes and waited a few seconds before speaking.

"That wasn't very nice," she said.

"I didn't mean it."

"You know I enjoyed it, Mark. You—"

"I'm sorry," I said.

She took a deep breath and let it out slowly. "Mark," she said, "what do I mean to you?"

"How do you mean?"

"What . . . what am I? I know you've had lots of women—"

"Not that many."

"But enough. Don't tell me how many. Don't tell me anything about them. I don't want to hear about them. I want to feel as though I'm the only woman and—"

She broke off suddenly and I wanted to tell her that she was the only one that mattered, that she made the others seem like vague memories from adolescent dreams. But she had something she wanted to get out and I waited for her to say it.

"Mark, am I just another lay? Just another woman who lies obligingly on her back with her knees pointed at the ceiling and who moves the right way and moans at the right time and—"

The words stopped again by themselves.

"You know you're not," I told her. She didn't seem to be listening to me. Her thoughts were a tangled mess that had trouble getting turned into words, and I knew it was leading up to a pitch that was against the few principles I have. She wanted me to live with her, with her paying the bills. And I didn't want it. It wouldn't work and I knew it instinctively.

"Mark, you mean a lot to me."

A pause.

"I'm not a tramp, Mark. I ... I haven't ... been with many other men. Just four, and I was married to one of them. I'm not trying to make myself sound like a paragon of virtue, but I want you to know that I slept with you because I wanted you."

"I know that."

"I like you very much, Mark. I don't want to talk about love because I'm not completely sure what love is and it's not especially important right now. I want to live with you and make love with you and be near you. I want to get to know you. Is that abnormal?"

"No."

Another pause, longer than the first.

"Stay here," she said. "Live with me. Get a job if you want to and pay me a few dollars a week for rent if it will make you feel better, but for God's sake don't leave me. I need you, Mark."

The tears were bottled up behind her eyes, ready to stream down her face if she let them.

But she wouldn't let them.

"Elaine," I said. "Elaine, honey."

I stood up and walked around the table to her, bending over to kiss the side of her neck. Then I straightened up and put a hand on each of her shoulders, looking down at her blonde hair.

"Elaine," I said. "Baby, it just wouldn't work. It wouldn't work at all."

"Why not?"

"I wouldn't be a man any more," I said. "I'd be another servant, and even if neither of us wanted it that way, that's how it would turn out. Pretty soon I'd quit whatever job I landed and then I'd be hanging around the house all day. You'd pay all the bills and I'd get used to the high life, and after a reasonable amount of time I'd be transformed into a gigolo. I don't want to be a gigolo, Elaine."

She didn't say anything.

"And you don't want me to, either. When that happened you wouldn't want me any more."

She stood up and turned to me, pushing the chair out of the way. She came into my arms, clutching fiercely at me, burying her face against my chest. Her hair was damp from the shower and smelled clean and fresh.

Then she pushed me away and turned from me. I reached for her but she wouldn't let me touch her. Her eyes turned back to me slowly and the beautiful sadness in them matched the record on the turntable in the other room.

"If you want to leave me," she said, "I don't suppose there's anything I can do to hold you."

"Don't talk like that."

"How do you want me to talk?" There was a slight edge of controlled hysteria in her voice.

"I don't want to leave you," I said. "And I'm not leaving you. I just plan to live somewhere else."

"I see," she said. "You'll live somewhere else, but we'll still see each other."

"Of course. Hell, you don't think I plan on going without you, do you? You mean a lot to me, Elaine."

It was the truth. She did.

"I see," she said again. "I see quite a bit now, Mark."

I looked at her.

"You don't want a woman," she said very slowly. "You want a whore."

"What—"

"A whore," she repeated. "A free whore but a whore just the same. Somebody you can sleep with but somebody who won't get in your way or take up your time or cut you off from your precious freedom. Somebody to come to when you feel like it, but somebody who won't be a bother to you."

"That's not what I mean!"

"Don't shout, Mark. And don't be so sure of it. Let me talk for a minute."

I let her talk.

"I'm not a whore, Mark."

I felt like pointing out to her that I already had a fairly good idea that she wasn't a whore, that I didn't want a whore to begin with and a few other things, but it was her turn at bat.

I kept my mouth shut.

"I'm not a whore and I don't think or relate like a whore. You've got it all figured out, haven't you? We'll be lovers and all, but you still expect me to sleep in an empty bed after you're gone and wake up in the morning without you next to me. We'll be lovers and we'll mean a lot to each other, but we won't get to know each other very well because we won't spend enough time with each other.

"Oh, we'll see each other. We'll see each other and I'll make some martinis and put on a record and we'll wind up in bed together. But that's not spending time together. After awhile it will become completely automatic, because no matter how good we are together—and we're better than I ever believed two people could possibly be, Mark—no matter how good we are, there has to be something more or it's no more significant than two dogs in somebody's back yard."

I got a mental picture at this point that I cannot possibly describe.

"Don't you see, Mark? You don't want to be a . . . a gigolo. No one's asking you to be one, for goodness sake. But you want me to be a slut and I don't want to be that either. I'm not the kind of woman who can settle for a man on a part-time basis. I'm not built that way."

She started to say something else but she didn't make it and came into my arms again with her face against my chest and her hair tickling my face. She had put in her turn at the plate and now she was handing me the bat, and I didn't know exactly what I was supposed to do with it. I could try swinging for the fences or settle for a sacrifice fly, but I had a strong hunch that neither alternative was going to satisfy either of us for very long.

She had a point. If I lived in a Third Avenue rooming house while she lived on Park Avenue we would have to call it quits in no time flat.

And I could hardly expect Elaine Rice, who had more money than God, to share my bed and board in Brokesville. Sex is sex is sex is sex, and I'm not knocking it by any stretch of the imagination, but all the glands in our hot little bodies wouldn't compensate for a scene like that. Elaine Rice on Third Avenue would be comparable to a diamond in a coal field. We just couldn't make it that way.

I suppose the smart thing at this point is to put your hat on your head and go home. Wham, bam, thank you, Ma'am and I'll see you around the campus. Goodbye Elaine, goodbye Miss Rice, so long and take care of yourself and thanks very much for the martinis and the Vivaldi and the Carelli and the Modern Jazz Quartet. And the scrambled eggs and coffee, plus the ride from Albany.

This was the smart thing, and there are times when this is also the easy and tasteful thing to do. Sally Austin, for instance—Sally Austin of the insatiable temperament and the boyish body with hips like a jackrabbit.

Nor was Sally the first. Men and women fall into the same

bed at the same time for a mélange of reasons, the most frequent and nearly logical being that they both feel like having a go at it. A one-night stand is usually enough under those circumstances, and there's no reason on earth to make a huge production out of parting.

This was different.

And that's what was giving me a quiet headache.

"Look," I whispered into all that blonde hair. "What the hell are we going to do?"

"I don't know." Her voice soft and cool, her lips rubbing against the front of my tee-shirt as she spoke the words.

"I suppose the obvious thing is to meet halfway," I suggested.

"I guess so,"

"Where's half way?"

"My way."

"Is this some new type of logic or are you just trying to prove you're a woman?"

"It's the truth."

"Sure."

"It is, Mark. Think about it for a minute."

I thought about it for a minute.

"Mark, your way is for you to see me only at bedtime. The opposite of that would be for you to live here with me picking up the tab for everything. You wouldn't work and we'd live a high old life, partying every night and never getting out of bed before noon. I'd like it that way, if you were the type of man who could go for an arrangement like that. But if you were that sort of guy I probably wouldn't like you."

The MJQ record ended and another one dropped on top of it. Sonny Rollins' "Freedom Suite". The girl had fine taste, believe me.

"So my way is in the middle."

"Explain."

"I've been trying to," she said, petulantly. "I've been trying to, but you're so afraid that little kids will run after you on the street shouting *gigolo* that I haven't been able to tell you a thing."

"Go ahead."

"You'll live here, with me. There's plenty of room in the apartment, more room than I could possibly take up all by myself, and—"

"Yeah, I know."

"Just shut up and listen to me. You'll live here, and you'll get a job and work, and you'll come home to me and we'll have dinner. You'll be living the same kind of life as you would if I didn't have any money, the only difference being that you'll be living in a slightly better place."

"Slightly? Try considerably."

She didn't say anything.

"And eating considerably better food," I went on.

"Is that so terrible?"

"Not terrible at all."

"We'll both have to make concessions," she said. "It's inevitable. This is a whacky sort of a thing between us and it's not the way things usually happen. But I think you'll agree it's worth a try."

"Of course it is."

"Then don't pout." She pecked at my lips and I grinned. I kissed her and she grinned. After a few minutes of that we were both grinning like a couple of idiots.

We didn't make love that night.

We could have, I suppose. But I didn't feel any monumental inner need to prove my virility, since I seriously doubted that it could be questioned after our performance earlier in the evening.

And we were both pretty much exhausted.

Besides, it was pretty goddamned pleasant just lying there in a good bed with clean sheets, holding the world's most beautiful woman in my arms. We talked for awhile, and it is an enjoyable experience indeed to lie very still with a naked woman pressed against you while the two of you carry on a light conversation.

I won't tell you what we talked about. It's none of your damned business.

After awhile we ran out of words and the bed became miraculously softer and the world spun around in exotic circles. We fell asleep in that position, lying on our sides with our arms around each other, and I dreamed pleasant dreams.

Waking up was delicious.

You see, we were ready for each other when we both came back to life at the same time. We didn't speak at all. Words were utterly unnecessary. We made love, and that is all that can be said about it—blind, pure love.

•   •   •

It started that afternoon.

Well, it had to. I knew it in the back of my mind when I agreed to the set-up the night before, and even then I must have realized that it was only a question of time before the world rolled off on its merry way to hell, the jolly old road with good intentions for paving stones.

It was Saturday, conveniently. It was Saturday, and the employment agencies were happily closed, so we stayed in bed until noon and did happy things.

While she was cooking breakfast—she was turning into quite the domestic type, by the way—I went to a newsstand on 34th Street and picked up a copy of the *Times*. I brought it back to the apartment, getting the same bland looks from the doorman and the elevator op, and I opened it to the HELP WANTED MALE section.

Seeing that the employment agencies and the office buildings have decided that Saturday ought to be a day of rest, the classifieds in the *Times* are considerably less in number than during the week. On Sunday there are tons of them, what with everybody ready to rush out and grab a job on Monday morn, but Saturday the whole list of HELP WANTED MALE, from ACCT to XRAY TCHNCN, took up somewhat less than half a page, even with all the silly ads for engineers.

Do you have any idea, by the way, how easy it is for an engineer to get a job? Pick up a copy of any paper from *Hobo News* to *Labor Action* and you'll get a fair idea. Good jobs, too. If I ever have any kids I will be sure they become engineers. More opportunities than you can shake a slide rule at, and it's frightening.

I wasn't an engineer, needless to say, and the whole picture looked pretty depressing, even when I stopped to take into consideration the fact that the whole picture generally looked depressing on a Saturday. Jobs were relatively scarce, pay was relatively low, and everything I saw was relatively unappealing.

Elaine pushed a stack of pancakes at me. It was a good tall stack and I smeared them with butter and doused them with real maple syrup. The syrup ran onto the sausages, those cute little breakfast sausages that you keep in the freezer and then brown in a pan for a minute or two and they're ready. I didn't mind—maple syrup and sausage is not the worst combination in the world, in case you never happened to try it.

The pancakes were light and fluffy and I dug into them, hardly noticing for the moment either the paper in front of me or the woman who had cooked the pancakes. I dissected a sausage with the side of my fork, speared it on the tines and popped it into my mouth.

Delicious.

So I said: "Delicious."

I went back to the obviously important tasks of finishing my breakfast and job hunting. The classifieds were beginning to bore me but the breakfast was getting all my attention, and I didn't even pay much attention to her the first time she said my name. I barely heard her, and the second time she said *Mark* I grunted something unintelligible.

"What kind of a job are you looking for?"

"I don't know."

"Don't you have anything in mind?"

"Only in a vague sort of a way. Something where I don't have to work more than eight hours a day—nice simple physical labor that'll bring me an easy seventy-five bucks a week or so without knocking me for a loop."

"Like what?"

"Hell, I don't know." I polished off the last forkful of pancake and bit my way into the last bite of sausage.

"Give me a for-instance."

"A for-instance?"

"Uh-huh."

"For instance like loading trucks."

She pursed her lips and looked as though she was thinking. I had a hunch that she wasn't. Nothing personal—it's just that I can't quite believe that people are thinking when they purse their lips. I think they do it so that they'll look as though they're thinking.

"Nothing other than heavy physical labor like that?"

I pursed my lips. "Not necessarily—it's just that the heavy stuff is more apt to pay seventy-five or better. I could be a counterman or something like that, or a sales clerk or such, but then my pay would run closer to fifty."

"I see," she said. "You'd rather make seventy-five than fifty."

I grinned. "Who wouldn't?"

"Mark—"

The hairs bristled along the back of my neck. It was a warning I should have heeded but didn't.

"Go ahead."

"Mark, wouldn't you rather make even more money?"

I didn't even answer that one.

"Say $150 a week instead of $75? And even more once you got into the swing of things?"

The long, full windup.

The stretch.

The pitch.

Taggert, you goddamned idiot, duck! It's coming straight for your head!

CHAPTER 4

She won, of course.

It was a long, hard, knock-'em-down battle that lasted a good two hours. No voices raised, no harsh words, no tears, no kicks in the groin. Just words and words and words that didn't stop and didn't let up, just cold logic that made its own brand of sense.

"Be a management trainee," she told me. "Get a job that starts you at a hundred a week and moves you right up to a good position. There are companies all over the city that would want a man like you. Why waste yourself at seventy-five when you can make more than that in a better job and do less work for it?"

I argued that I didn't want to be a management trainee or a junior executive or anything else like that.

"What are you afraid of?" she taunted. "A job like that will give you a chance to use your brains instead of your muscles. Don't you want a chance to be somebody? You don't want to hold lousy jobs forever, do you?"

I told her the companies wouldn't want a guy like me.

"Of course they will," she countered. "You're being silly. You're smart and you've been around so that you're a good deal more mature than the average run-of-the-mill applicant. You've got a stable personality and a good mind and more than enough general experience to do the job properly. How many other applicants have been as many places as you have and held as many jobs? You'd be a natural for something like that, Mark."

I told her I didn't have an college education and that every ad of the type she was talking about clearly specified that they were interested in college grads. It seemed at the time like an unanswerable argument.

She had an answer, natch.

"You've got a college education," she said. "You don't have a degree, but you know more than the idiots who have degrees coming out of their ears. If you tell whoever hires you that you have a diploma he'll never know the difference."

I stared at her.

"Of course," she said. "They'd hardly stop to check it out. Tell them you have a bachelor's degree from Clifton College. Have you ever heard of Clifton College?"

I hadn't.

"Neither has anybody else," she said. "There is no Clifton College. But if you tell them you graduated five years ago from Clifton College in Clifton, Ohio with a bachelor's in . . . what do you know a lot about?"

I shrugged. Then I told her what I knew a lot about.

"That's fine," she said, "but I don't think you could convince them that Clifton gave degrees in sex. How about history or something like that?"

I shrugged again.

"That sounds good," she decided. "A history major. A nice level-headed field, but one which doesn't lead to any set type of work outside of teaching. So you'll tell them you don't want to teach because you want a position with more contact with the real competitive world than you can get in the groves of Academe and they'll be properly impressed."

"Elaine—"

She was getting carried away with the bit and there was no stopping her now, not while the idea was blazing away so brilliantly in her pretty little head. She doped out the precise approach and gave me my full background—drifting the past few years because I wanted to get as wide a knowledge of people and places as possible, now ready to settle down and interested in a spot with a solid, reputable company, a spot loaded with respectability and security, a spot where I could play my role as a functioning member of a solid, hard-hitting team.

It was a good bit, the whole philosophy of the Organization Man boiled down and easily digestible. I suggested sarcastically that we ought to move to Connecticut to fit the address with the personality and she damn near took me seriously. Then she realized that I was kidding and flashed me a quick, disapproving, *don't you realize this is something that affects your whole future* glance.

I shut up and listened to her.

We went over values. I was supposed to be a guy who liked money very much, but one who placed security and teamsmanship ahead of a quick plunge for a fast buck. My chief goal in life was a wife and kids and a house in some part of Suburbia, catching the 8:02 to the office every morning, catching the 5:17 back to Nowheresville, Connecticut every evening, getting picked up at the station by my ever-loving wife who was driving our ever-loving station wagon, and so on into the night. I asked her very seriously how many times a week I should tell them I want to make love to my ever-loving wife and she frowned at me.

I didn't want the job. I never had wanted one of those team-playing deals because I never could stand the thought of living that type of life. Some guys want it—that's their business, and although I get very nasty and sarcastic when anybody talks Organization Man style, it's a good life if you're the type of person who's cut out for it.

I'm not. I don't like working for a team. I like working for myself, because as far as I am concerned I am the most important person in the world. Anybody who thinks somebody else is more important than himself is either a liar or an idiot or a saint. I'm most important to me, and you're most important to you, and that's the way it ought to be when you stop to think about it for a few minutes or so. This doesn't mean that the Golden Rule is a lot of hogwash; it doesn't mean that the best way to live your life is to put knives in other backs while you keep your own pressed to the wall. Looking out for Number One is no more and no less than simple arithmetic.

But she kept on talking. She told me that once I got the job I could start pushing my way on up the ladder. I'd be keeping up this team-playing surface, but actually I'd be climbing the ladder to success with the bodies of my fellow team-mates as the rungs on the ladder. Listening to Elaine, it seemed quite plausible to conjecture that in a year or so I'd be making ten grand a year, and in ten years I'd be making seventy-five grand a year, and in fifteen years I'd own the company and sell it to DuPont at a profit.

Sure.

I asked her just one question. I asked her why in the world I should do the whole bit.

It seemed to me like a very legitimate question. After all, she was asking me to alter my whole pattern of living completely, change my goals and submerge my own identity. It seemed that I ought to have a reason before I gave up being Mark Taggert and became somebody else entirely. Just to be able to reassure myself, if nothing else.

She gave me reasons. And one of the reasons, one that seemed to make a little more sense than the others, which made very little sense at all, was something like this: We were trying to keep us together. We were trying to do this without turning one Mark Taggert into a gigolo. The less money Mark Taggert had, the greater his propensity to become a gigolo. The more respectable said Mark Taggert became and the fatter his wallet grew, the less propensity he had to rely on one Elaine Rice for support.

Well, what did I want? I boiled it down to this: I wanted her, but I also wanted to be able to look myself in the eye without turning to stone.

Solution: Do like the lady tells you.

So I agreed for the second time in two days. Tomorrow, she decided for me, I would pick up a *Times* and we would really go over those ads. She'd help me phony a résumé for whatever poor

bastards we would pick out as a target and it would be onward
and upward to new and greater heights. Then I kissed her, more
out of relief that we were through with this nonsense for a day at
least, and the kiss turned into an embrace and the embrace turned
into a pretty passionate involvement, and a few minutes later we
were in the bedroom and taking another trip to Heaven together.

It was after the love bout and the post-love-bout shower that she
hit me over the head with a mallet. She did it in a straight and un-
assuming manner, bring the mallet up over her head and knocking me into the floor with it.

"Better get dressed," she said. "We have to go shopping."

"What for?"

"Clothes," she said.

"I wouldn't be much help. I don't know much about women's
clothing, and no matter how you're dressed you'll look good to
me." I winked lewdly and smacked my lips.

"They're not women's clothes."

"You're suddenly a transvestite?"

"Don't be difficult, Mark. We have to get some clothes for
you."

"I *have* clothes."

She didn't appear to have heard me but went right on talking,
mostly to herself, her voice low and her eyes focused on my belt
buckle. "You'll need a suit or two," she said. "And at least two
sport jackets and half a dozen shirts—better make that ten to a

dozen. And two decent pairs of shoes and a couple belts and ties and some socks and—"

"Hey!"

"Wait a minute," she had the nerve to say. "I want to go over this in my head first. I suppose you'll need a topcoat as well, and some other accessories, and—"

"Elaine."

My voice was flat and very dead and it stopped her cold. She looked up at me, bewildered.

"Elaine, I can't afford clothes right now."

"What?"

"I have about fifty bucks," I said, "and even if I went shopping in the Rivington Street flea market I couldn't buy half of what you just got finished babbling about. So you can stop right there and not worry about making up a list, because—"

"I know you can't afford it, Mark."

"And?"

"And I *can* afford it. So don't start acting like somebody's poor relation."

"Look, Elaine."

"You look. You have to be dressed properly if you want to get anywhere. You can't walk into an executive position in a pair of khakis and a tee-shirt, and you can't get to the top of any firm with old tennis shoes on your feet."

"If it'll make you happy," I said, "I'll buy a new pair of tennis shoes."

"Don't talk like an idiot."

"Elaine, I'm not going to let you buy clothes for me."

And the argument started again, and I didn't have the chance of an ice cube in Hell. She had logic on her side now—I obviously had agreed to take the kind of job she suggested, and I obviously couldn't without decent clothing on my back, and she obviously was going to win the argument.

She did.

Obviously.

Well, she wasn't going to *buy* clothes for me, not exactly. She was going to *loan* me the money, and I was going to pay her back when I had a chance. A semantic difference, but as far as I could see it boiled down to her laying out the money with no guarantee she would see it again, no interest, no time limit on the loan— nothing but the pleasure and privilege of seeing her man walk around well dressed.

I gave in, though. But she didn't leave it there—she kept on going until I agreed that it was better this way, and she did such a thorough job of brainwashing me that I was all in favor of it by the time she was through. Hell, I hadn't been dressed decently in a while. It might be fun—sort of a new experience, more or less.

We dressed and walked over to the menswear shops on Broadway in the upper Thirties. There's a whole slew of them there in the heart of the garment district and they're all good and all expensive. I told her 14th Street would be as good and she told me that the better I was outfitted the better my chances would be, and by this time I had decided that it was her money and she could call the shots. A dangerous decision, by the way.

It was her money and she called the shots. We bought everything in one place on the theory that it was better to have a wardrobe all of a piece, so to speak. The place we so honored was a tiny emporium called Brinsley's, a hole in the wall with no price tags on the clothing in the window. That's always a clue—when they leave the tags off on the window display you know their prices are sky high.

And they were. The suit she picked out for me was a dark-blue affair with narrow stripes, a very fashionable thing indeed, with a very fashionable price tag attesting that it would set her back $119.95. The three pairs of slacks were of charcoal brown, charcoal grey and Cambridge grey flannel and hovered around twenty bucks per.

The sport jackets—two of them, yet—were in the classy neighborhood of a yard for the two. One was a fairly garish tweed, loud and showy but so well designed and well made that it carried it off perfectly. The other was a tweed as well but a more subdued one. I liked them both.

A black alligator belt.

Monogrammed handkerchiefs. Irish linen, too.

White oxford-cloth shirts with button-down collars.

Blue oxford-cloth shirts with button-down collars.

Striped oxford-cloth shirts with button-down collars.

Paisley shirts with tab collars.

Ties.

Socks.

Cuff links.

Tie clips.

I drew the line at underwear, damn it. Enough is enough, and I didn't think there would be too many important business conferences going on in the Men's Room where somebody big would find out that my underwear did not happen to come from Brinsley's exclusive Store For Men.

The total bill came to a thoroughly astronomical figure, something like the federal defense budget. She paid it on the spot in cash and even Brinsley was a little awed. We got out of the store with his fervent promise to deliver the stuff by Tuesday at the latest ringing in our ears and made it across the street to the shoe store, where we picked out three pairs of shoes ranging from $19.85 to $23.90 a pair. This didn't awe me any more. I was getting used to it.

The next afternoon was Sunday and she pounced on the *Times* the minute I got in the door with it. We went through the ads with a fine-tooth comb and circled the ones that looked interesting. I didn't think any of them looked particularly interesting, but she was glowing with the excitement of the whole thing and I was carried along with her to a degree. This was one happy doll, this Elaine Rice, this mistress of mine. Her eyes were shining as she ran her fingers up and down the HELP WANTED MALE ads, talking very swiftly under her breath and being very active and busy about it all.

I had her figured out, sort of. It wasn't just whatever she felt for me that had her so hot to go, though that of course played a large part in it. It was also the fact that it gave her something to do, something that could prove to be very fascinating. She had it all set up for me to rise to the top of some heap or other, and she would be at my side all the way, helping and prodding and planning, rising with me vicariously like the loving helpmates you read about in the stories in the slick magazines, if you have the stomach to read those stories.

Sunday was planning and narrowing the field and drafting a résumé.

Monday was writing letters to those few firms that wanted applications by mail, and Monday was also getting the story ready and rehearsing it.

Tuesday was personality day—how I should smile, how I should react, how I should think and feel and how much I should sweat. Everything—Elaine Rice was a very thorough and exacting little doll.

Tuesday was also the day the clothes came. I dressed myself up just to see how I would look in a pair of grey flannels and the louder of the two sport jackets, with a blue shirt and black Italian-style shoes and argyle socks and a foulard tie with the tie clip holding it in place.

She told me I looked wonderful.

I looked at myself in the mirror to check and I almost had to agree with her. The guy in the mirror didn't look much like Mark Taggert at all. The guy in the mirror was Joe Sophistication, a neat suave son of a bitch dressed like something out of *Esquire*, a fashion-plate with his face and neck fashionably tanned, with hair cropped close to head in a fashionable crew cut, with fingernails believe-it-or-not professionally manicured. The hair-cut-and-manicure bit had been one of Monday's projects, and while it felt a little bit ridiculous to sit in a chair while a pretty girl with bouncing breasts prodded my cuticles with an orangewood stick and buffed them with something else and in various other ways fooled around with my hands, I had to admit that the overall effect was worth all the nonsense.

We celebrated with dinner in a French restaurant in the east Fifties. If you have never supped in a French restaurant in the east Fifties I have nothing but pity for you. I had never done so, and it was with an inexplicable amount of jollity that I did.

This particular restaurant was on 53rd Street just off Fifth Avenue. We started with dry Gibsons and worked our way through appetizers and soups to the main course, which was guinea hen with wild rice for her and duck in tangerine sauce for me.

Then we still felt in a celebratish mood, so we went to a little jazz club on Hudson Street where we sat and listened to Tristano and Konitz for three hours for less than the dessert had cost us in the French place. Tristano played very far out sounds on the piano that came from the happy little world inhabited by Lennie Tristano all alone by himself, and Konitz made obligingly pleasant saxophone conversation, and the drinks were good and the company in the person of my lovely Elaine was delightful.

Then we went home, and we still felt in a celebratish mood.

So we made love.

CHAPTER 5

Inside of ten days I had the job I wanted.

It was amazingly simple, so simple that I found it pretty hard to believe. Evidently if it appears that you're prosperous enough so that you're a damn fool to want the job, the boss finds it impossible to turn you down. I walked in with my suit and my shoes and my shirt and tie and tie clip and he practically handed me the keys to the place and told me to take over. It was ridiculous, and it was fun, and I was employed.

I was traffic manager for Matterhorn Press, a textbook house. I was taking home $125 for an eight-hour-a-day, forty-hour week, sitting in a swivel chair with a cute brunette with unbelievable breasts for a secretary. An office of my own, and any day now some jerk would come along and paint *Mark Taggert* on the door.

Incredible!

"You're just the man I've been looking for," the boss told me. He was a fat little guy named Marty Jukovsky, with a round face and big round eyes and a soft look to him that didn't fit in with the fact that he had taken a broken-down bible-and-dictionary house and turned it into the second largest textbook outfit in the country.

"Just the man," he said again, this time taking the cigar out of his mouth and poking holes in the air with it for emphasis. "Old enough so that you know what the hell you're doing. Young enough so that you can learn. Brains in your head. Feet on the ground. Solid."

He puffed on the cigar and blew smoke at me.

"Something else, too," he said. "Quality. Listen to me, I can sense it when a guy has quality. It makes a difference. You take these average Joes—" his hand waved the cigar at the office in general. There were, at the moment, no average Joes to be seen "—they got nothing. No sense, no poise, no quality. You can go a long ways."

I felt like telling him that the quality I had cost a few hundred dollars at Brinsley's but I kept my mouth shut. If the cover was going to sell him there was no point in opening the book and giving him a look at the table of contents. Hell, if I had come in with the khakis and tee-shirt he wouldn't have hired me to wrap packages in his stock room.

"This other idiot," he said. "This moron I had for a traffic manager, every order that came in he fouled it up. Would you believe me if I told you he sent fifty calculus texts to a grammar school in Oak Falls? Oak Falls, Montana? Calculus texts, yet. So the third grade could learn from differential and integral calculus, whatever in hell that is. The principal out there wrote she thought there must have been an error of some sort. Hah!"

I wondered vaguely whether he had ever had any dealings

with Clifton College, my fictitious alma mater. It was a shame the place didn't exist. What the hell—maybe I'd send them a load of calc texts one of these days.

"Ever do anything like traffic?"

"Not exactly," I said. *Not exactly.* The only thing I ever did like traffic was jaywalk across 42nd Street.

"Doesn't matter," he said. "Doesn't make a bit of difference. You—I can tell with you. You'll pick it up real fast. Nothing to it."

He was right—that was the funny part of it. The nice and wonderful thing about a job like traffic managing is that it takes no appreciable talent whatsoever. Mr. Jukovsky was dead right there. I learned nearly all there was to know about the job the first day and got out all the necessary orders, shipping Matterhorn textbooks all over the damned country.

It was easier than slinging hash, easier than selling insurance, easier than helping Mike Corrigan make roads. All you needed was a brain, and it didn't have to be a particularly clever or active brain. You just had to be able to read the orders, figure out the right way to fill them, the time to ship and what shipping method to use. Anybody who can figure out that you don't send letters airmail from Manhattan to the Bronx can handle the job.

And so here I was, sitting behind a heavy modern looking desk in a swivel chair with coasters and looking across the office at my chesty secretary and waiting for the jerk to come and paint my name on the door. Right now the door said Lester Swift on it, and since good old Les was the bonehead who had managed to foul up Matterhorn Press a good sixteen ways, and since his orders always got things to the wrong place at the wrong time, I figured his last name wasn't particularly suitable. I also figured he was something of a jackass, and I didn't especially want his damned name on my door.

As a matter of fact, I had just finished dictating a letter to a college book store somewhere in Iowa, apologizing profusely for the fact that Les, the bonehead, had sent their books to some place in Idaho. Dictating was a brand new experience and lots of fun, sitting in my chair with my feet up on the desk and drawling the words out to Miss Simmons. At first the whole notion of dictating seemed terrifying, and I started off by trying to pace the room and dictate like the top executives in the movies. It didn't work. Now I just sat back and talked, and when the letter was neatly typed on Matterhorn Press stationery I signed it. It was easier than falling off a desert.

That's what I told Miss Simmons.

"But you can't fall off a desert."

"That's it," I said.

"Huh?"

"That's what makes it so much easier."

She laughed uneasily and I looked at her. Her damned typewriter was in the way and I couldn't get a look at the best part of her, but I could see her face and it was almost as much fun to look at her face as it was to sort of stare unbelievingly at her chest.

Her name was Sara Simmons and she was as young as she looked, which was about 21. Her hair was jet black and it hung in little ringlets, framing a pretty face with high cheekbones and a cute little pug nose. She smiled often when she was talking or listening, but when I glanced at her while she was opening mail or typing a letter or doing any one of a number of absurd little tasks, her face was always sober and demure. She didn't use rouge or eyeshadow or any of the glop that women louse up their faces with—just a touch of lipstick that made her lips a little more red.

She finished what she was typing and pushed the typewriter over to one side. It was a good thing she did; I was about ready to walk over there and give the machine a shove myself. Now I could look at her, and it was a pleasure, believe me. The largest breasts in the world, bar none—and they had to be hers because nobody in the world would dare make falsies that size.

Her white cotton blouse was loose at the waist. It couldn't help being loose at the waist. If it had fit that slender waist properly, her breasts would have broken through.

Laboriously I dragged my mind back to the job of managing traffic for Matterhorn.

"What's next?"

She smiled cheerily. "Nothing, Mr. Taggert."

"Nothing?"

"Nothing that I can find. My goodness, when Mr. Swift was here we were always piled up with work. But you've got everything finished already and the day isn't anywhere near over."

I glanced at my watch. The day, to be exact, was an hour and a half from being over.

Work all done. Well, that gave me a little while to play games, and the first thing to do was break her of the *Mr. Taggert* habit. They could paint that on the door if they wanted to, but I was damned if I would make my secretary call me by my last name. Especially when she looked like Sara Simmons.

"Miss Simmons?"

She looked up.

"What did you used to call Swift?"

"Call him?"

"Yeah—did you call him Les or Lester?"

"Oh—why, I called him Mr. Swift. Why?"

"I guess it figures," I said, half to her and half for my own satisfaction. "I suppose if I had to choose between being called Les or Lester I'd pick Mr. Swift."

She was looking at me with a strange look in her eye, as if perhaps I was working too hard and it had done something serious to the inside of my head. I decided to set her little mind at ease.

"I just wanted to stop you from calling me by my last name," I said. "I'm not Mr. Taggert. My father was Mr. Taggert. My name is Mark."

"Mark," she said. Testing it, rolling it on her tongue.

"And you're Sara."

"That's right."

"Sara," I said in a fatherly tone, "we have roughly an hour and a half to kill. How do you think we ought to go about slaying it?"

"I don't think I understand, Mr. Taggert."

"Mark," I corrected.

"Mark," she repeated.

"That's it," I said. "Now what in the devil are we going to do with the rest of the afternoon?"

"I don't know."

I thought fleetingly that her breasts might owe their size to the fact that that was where she kept her brains. No, that was being unfair. She had a head on her shoulders, and she was efficient and cool and polished when she was working, which was all the time up until now. She was just flustered, evidently.

"Sara," I said, "the intelligent thing for us to do would be to go out of this stuffy little hole and drown ourselves in gin. But I don't think Mr. Jukovsky would approve."

"He probably wouldn't."

"Let's talk, or you talk—I'm sick of talking. I've been talking all day. Talk!"

"What—"

"Talk!" I half shouted. I was beginning to get some sadistic pleasure out of keeping the poor girl perpetually dizzy.

"What should I talk about?"

"Anything. You, your home town. Where you live. Your family. What the hell do I care what you talk about just so long as you talk!"

By this time I had managed to fake one hell of a rage and she was on the point of a crack up, so I got out of my chair and walked over to her and started laughing, and then apologized for torturing her, and finally got a merry little smile out of her. I also got a nice close look at the front of her blouse and had to struggle to keep my hands at my sides.

Then I went back to my chair and sat down while she talked. Once she got going she talked a blue streak and it was ten after five before we realized it. She hailed from the town of Hustead, a small town in Ohio near Dayton, and she attended college at a place called Trundleberg College, a name which sounded infinitely less plausible than Clifton. Proving, if nothing else, that truth is a good deal stranger than fiction.

She was born in Hustead, and she lived all her life in Hustead except for the four years spent in (shudder) Trundleberg and the year or so she had been in New York. The school such as it was, must have made a deep impression on her; she used the word *Trundleberg* three times in the same involved sentence.

"Where did they get the name?" I wanted to know.

"The man who founded it was named Trundleberg."

"What was his first name?"

"Clarence," she said.

It figured.

She went on. She had two brothers and a sister, and the sister was going to Trundleberg right now. The damned word came up constantly.

I interrupted her again.

"Sara," I said, "did Trundleberg have a football team?"

"Well . . . sort of."

"Sort of?"

"It wasn't much of a team," she explained. "They couldn't afford uniforms so they used old sweatshirts, and for cleats they took thumbtacks and struck them through the bottoms of their shoes, and—"

"Did they have a nickname for the team?"

"A nickname?"

"Yeah, you know. Like the New York Yankees, or the Michigan Wolverines, or like that."

"Oh," she said.

"I just wondered."

They had a name they used some of the time," she said. "It was sort of a funny name."

"What was it?"

"The Thunderbirds."

"The Trundleberg Thunderbirds?"

She nodded solemnly and her big beautiful breasts bobbed up and down.

When I left the office I was tired, tired enough to splurge a buck on a cab to the apartment. I felt very fine, very happy and prosperous as I stepped out of the cab on Park Avenue and slipped a bill to the driver. By the time I walked up the steps and across the lobby to the elevator I wasn't tired any more. My step was lively and I was whistling a tune, and I smiled at the elevator op when he told me it was a nice day. I smiled again when he let me out of the car and smiled my way down the hallway to the apartment.

What the hell, I was a pretty lucky guy. How many Joes do you know with a Trundleberg grad for a secretary? And did a busty girl ever reveal to you the existence of the so-help-me Trundleberg Thunderbirds?

Not to mention $125 a week. Not to mention a posh pad on Park Avenue. Not to mention the most beautiful woman in the world sharing my bed.

Or did I have it backwards? Come to think of it, she wasn't sharing my bed. I was sharing her bed. There was a difference, a quiet difference but an eminently tangible one. It was her bed and her apartment, and without her I wouldn't be earning the yard-and-a-quarter a week either.

I stifled the notion—it was making me feel lousy again, and I was feeling too good to start feeling lousy. I gave the buzzer a nudge to give her time to freshen up—or to hide her lover in the closet if she happened to be committing adultery. I counted to ten by fives and unlocked the door just as she was reaching to open it.

My Elaine. My beautiful Elaine, fresh and lovely and big and beautiful. I reached out for her and held her and kissed her and she snuggled up against me. I released her and stepped inside, and she disappeared for a moment and came back with a pair of martinis for us. I took one from her and we sat side by side on the couch with the martinis, and I remembered how it was exactly the same as the first night and yet totally different.

The music this time was a Bach suite for orchestra. I listened to it for a moment admiringly, took a sip of my drink and smacked my lips, and turned to gaze into the eyes of my beloved.

"Hey!" I said. "Where are you going?"

She was dressed to the teeth in a blue sack-type dress that didn't look at all like a sack now that it had her inside it. It wasn't exactly the sort of outfit to sweat over a hot stove in. And she didn't look at all as though she'd been sweating over a hot stove.

"I'm going with you," she said. "Where else would I be going?"

"Let me rephrase the question. Where are *we* going?"

"Out."

"That," I said, "is relatively obvious. Where?"

"Dinner."

I thought about that for a second or two. "Honey," I said, "we've been going out too much. Spending too much money on dinners."

"Do you think so?"

I nodded. "We were out for dinner four nights last week and two nights this week already. It wouldn't be so bad if we were going to inexpensive places, but we've been averaging about twelve bucks a meal what with a drink before and the tip. Now—"

"We can afford it, Mark."

"Maybe you can afford it. I can't, and now that I've got a job I think we ought to start thinking about living on my salary. And we can't do that if—"

"Mark."

Something in her voice made me stop.

"Mark, I've been doing a lot of thinking."

"Go ahead."

"I don't know just how to say this."

I didn't say anything. When somebody doesn't know just how to say something, the best thing to do is shut up and let her figure out a way. She set her drink down on the coffee table and rested her chin on one hand with a deep-in-thought expression on her face. She stayed that way for about a minute while I let myself get a little bit lost in the Bach suite. It's nice stuff to get lost in—more complex than the Vivaldi but still easy to listen to.

"Mark."

I tore myself away from the Bach.

"Mark, I'm afraid we're not going to be able to live on your salary."

I had some things to say to that but it was obvious that she wasn't through yet. I waited for her to go on.

"I've begun to realize something," she said. "Mark, I have an . . . enormous amount of money. The bulk of it is invested in a solid mutual fund that brings me an income of between seventy and eighty thousand dollars a year. There's also some more in government bonds and a little more in slightly more speculative securities. The result is that I have a . . . well, a pretty huge income, plus a principal that increases every year."

"I wish you didn't have it."

"So do I."

"But you do. And you can't just chuck it in the ashcan, can you?"

"I guess not."

Simultaneously we each raised our glasses to our lips and drained our drinks. Simultaneously we set our glasses down on the coffee table and fell into each other's arms. I loved her at that moment more than I had ever loved her before, loved her with the desperate and horrible knowledge that we were going to lose each other. I kissed her forehead, the nape of her neck, the tip of her nose. Sexless, loving kisses.

I loved her.

I hated her money.

CHAPTER 6

There was no hurry this time, no mad rush like the first time. I walked to the record player and pressed the button to reject the record. The tone arm came to a stop, stood up, looked around bewildered and went back to sit down where it belonged. Then I flipped a switch and the turntable stopped revolving.

I took the record, which turned out to be Bach's "Suite No. 2", and slipped it into its jacket. I returned it to the cabinet.

Meanwhile Elaine had returned the martini glasses to the sink and returned herself to the bedroom. When I got there she was already in bed, her clothes hung up and put away and her body outlined beneath the sheet.

I undressed methodically. I hung up my suit, draped my shirt over the back of a chair, put my socks in my shoes and my underwear on the chair.

Then I joined her in the bed.

No air of mystery. No candles burning, no soft music, nothing secret and nothing silent. Our lovemaking was simple and unadorned. We had no ornaments for it this time, no special wrappings to invest it with magical properties.

All we had was our love.

And it didn't seem to be enough.

When I took her in my arms her mouth was moist against my cheek. She said my name in a frightened little-girl voice and threw her arms around my neck like a drowning man reaching out to strangle his rescuer, holding me tight and hard against her.

"Mark, I'm afraid. I'm terrified, Mark."

"Don't be afraid."

I rubbed the palm of my hand over her body. Her flesh quivered under my touch.

"Mark, I don't want you to leave me. I . . . I couldn't stand it."

Tears once more in the corners of her eyes. But they were tears that would never spill, tears that would never run down her face, tears that would never leave a salty trail from her beautiful eyes to her beautiful chin. She had her tears very well disciplined.

"Mark—"

My lips found the valley between her breasts. I kissed the unbearably soft skin there and her arm stole around me and her hand rubbed the small of my back.

"I love you, Mark."

The skin on the underside of her breasts was softer and smoother still. Her flesh was very tender there, very sensitive, and she began to squirm and writhe a little beneath me.

"Mark, I love you."

"I love you, Elaine."

Her voice strained when she spoke, strained with passion and love and all the other mixed-up emotions, and my hand moved with a will of its own.

"So funny," she said. "So funny."

"What's funny?"

"All funny. Me—I'm funny. I wasn't going to let myself fall in love, Mark. I stopped believing in love. I wanted you and I thought that was all there had to be. But now I'm going to lose you."

I opened my mouth to say something. I changed my mind and kept my mouth shut.

"Don't say anything," she said. Now her voice was so small and strained I could hardly recognize it. "Don't tell me anything different, Mark. And don't try to explain."

My mouth kissed her and my hand held her. She was warm for me, warm and moist for me, and we loved each other with the depth and emotion of tragedy.

"It was just a mess, Mark. Just a mess from start to finish. I want you now more than I ever did and you want me, and you're going to leave me and I don't want you to. I want you to stay, I want so much for you to stay, I want it more than I ever wanted anything and all the wanting in the world isn't going to do me any good and I know it. You're going to go and in the morning you'll be gone and it will be all over and done with, and I don't want it to happen."

I loved her. I loved her so much it was killing me, loved her deeply and painfully.

"Mark—"

"I love you."

"Then love me, Mark. Make me forget that you're leaving me. Make me forget who I am and where I am and everything except that you're with me and we're in love.

"Love me hard, Mark. Hurt me. Do everything to me because this is the last time and I don't want it to be the last time because I . . . I . . . I—"

When her voice broke I knew she had said all she was going to say.

Her breathing was hoarse, her eyes closed, her face drawn. With my hand on her breast I could feel the throbbing of her heart. Her heart was racing, beating hard and missing beats.

We came to the top of the world together. She was gripping me close and holding onto me with all the superhuman strength that love and fear inspire.

A release.

Not the peace that love can bring. Not full relaxation, with everything calm and beautiful and good and two bodies lying together bathing in their own love.

Not that.

Just a release, just a certain amount of tension dispelled while a certain amount yet remained. Just a release, just a break in the weather, just a letting go of muscles and nerves and tendons.

Just a release.

Just her finger drawing infinitesimal circles in the matted hair of my chest and her face buried in the softness of her pillow.

• • •

I dressed as methodically as I had undressed. I put on my underwear and my socks, my shirt and my suit and my shoes. I dressed quite rapidly, all in all, and while I dressed she lay on the bed face downward, her body gleaming in its nakedness and her blonde hair shining up at me, glowing like a blast furnace.

When I had finished dressing I found an old suitcase of hers in the closet. One of the hinges was busted and the leather was scratched in spots, and burned in one place where some dolt had gotten careless with a cigarette. It was good enough for me and it was one she would be able to get along without, so I took it and set it down on the chair and opened it up.

I started throwing clothes in it. I didn't exactly *throw* them in, as a matter of fact, because when you buy your clothes at Brinsley's you do not throw them. You place them, and you place them gently and with loving care.

I placed my wardrobe gently and with loving care in the suitcase. I packed everything I owned—what didn't fit in the suitcase went into the laundry bag. Packing a suitcase is not exactly my strong point, which is one of the reasons I had always stuck to a laundry bag or an old pillow case in the past. Any halfass can pack a laundry bag—all you do is take things and put them into it. With a suitcase you have to call upon all the things you didn't learn in that solid geometry class back in high school. It's an arduous process.

It took time, as is the case with the usual run of arduous processes. And because it took time I felt like leaving the clothing and just getting the hell out. It hurt, standing there and packing while the woman you loved was lying silent and motionless and sad on the bed a few feet away from you. It hurt like hell.

When I finally had the suitcase shut and the locks snapped I walked over to the bed and sat down on the edge of it. I didn't touch her; I had a feeling she didn't want to be touched, not just then. What we had done was the end, the ultimate. It would be better to leave it that way, finished, over with. Touching her or kissing her would only make things just that much worse, would only make the break that much harder for both of us to bear.

"Elaine?"

She didn't answer me.

"I'm going now, Elaine."

She rolled over, propping herself up with one arm. Her eyes were red and swollen but not from crying. She hadn't cried, but the effort of holding back tears that wanted to flow had made her face all puffed up and messy.

I wanted to kiss those red eyes.

"I've got my stuff all packed," I said instead. "I'll leave in a minute or two."

"Can't you . . . can't you stay until morning?"

"It's better this way."

"I suppose so. But waking all alone without you here next to me after I've gotten so used to you—"

She still didn't cry. I almost wished she would. Maybe if she could cry I could stay, maybe if the tears would spill from her eyes our love would be enough to push everything else out of the way.

But she didn't cry.

I stood up woodenly and picked up my suitcase and my laundry bag. When I turned to her again her eyes were staring vacantly at me. She looked as though she was struggling to say something.

I waited.

"I love you," she said.

Her voice was a whisper, less than a whisper. Her voice was the wind on a windless day, the song of birds when no birds sing. Her voice was a screaming silence, and it shrieked at me so shrill and loud that I could barely hear it.

Her voice was the voice of the dead.

I left her there, and with my laundry bag slung over my left shoulder and my suitcase dangling from my right hand I walked out of the apartment, down the hallway to the elevator. I leaned on the button.

The elevator doors swung open after a minute or so and I stepped into the car. They'd switched ops since I had come upstairs, and this one was a big change from the youngster with the curly black hair who had whisked me upstairs. This guy had bags under his eyes that looked heavier than the ones I was carrying. His hair was grey and thin and he didn't go to a very good barber because it was a mess. He had managed to cut himself shaving and his face was a white blob dotted with red marks on his chin and neck.

He looked like I felt.

I didn't say good night to the poor bastard because it would have been wasted on both of us. I left him without a word, left the building without a word, and caught a cab in front. I gave the hack the address of a residential hotel in the west Forties.

The hotel was on 46th Street between Sixth and Seventh—not the world's best hotel by a long shot but not the worst in the world either. A decent medium-priced flop. I dragged myself to the desk and recognized the clerk, a shabby little guy named Moe. I had put up at the hotel, Hotel Touraine by name, about a year or so before.

Moe recognized me. We exchanged a word about old times, a brief word because I had talked to him maybe twice during the time I was living at the Touraine, and he showed me a room with a private bath. Nothing particularly plush, nothing like the apartment I had just finished walking out of, but the furniture was solid and the floor was clean and the bed was firm, and what the hell did I expect?

I took the room. It was $24.50 a week, which is not quite as high as it might sound because hotels in New York are high as a junkie after a good score. On my one-and-a-quarter a week I could afford it, and with the location I had a walk to work instead of a bus ride.

I unpacked. I'm better at unpacking than I am at packing, which is not surprising since it takes no particular skill to unpack. I did a neat job, hanging my clothes in the closet or putting them in a drawer in the bureau depending upon where they belonged. I changed from the suit jacket to the loud sport jacket, elevatored back down to the main floor in a self-service elevator that made me feel lonely, left my key with Moe and walked out into the night.

Then I did what any normal human being in the same set of circumstances would do.

The bar was located on Amsterdam Avenue at 84th Street.

As far as I am concerned, there is only one way in the world to go about quiet, solitary, serious drinking. This type of drinking must be done in an Irish bar and must involve imbibing impressive quantities of Irish whiskey. Martinis make good sense before dinner, and beer goes good when you're in a convivial mood, but serious drinking virtually demands Irish whiskey in an Irish bar.

This Irish bar was named McSwiney's. There was nobody named McSwiney connected with the bar and never had been. McSwiney was one Terence McSwiney, a hero of the Easter Risings of 1619 who was captured by the British, then jailed, and who starved himself to death on a monumental hunger strike. The original owner of McSwiney's was a guy by the name of Padraic Leary, and Leary was enough of an admirer of McSwiney to name his establishment after him.

It was an Irish bar all the way. No television set to hypnotize you into a drowsy state. No jukebox to irritate the people who had a reason for drinking. No snappy chatter, no floozies looking for pick-ups, no dancing and no dames and no ornamentation.

The window was painted a solid green and you couldn't see in from the outside. McSWINEY'S was painted on the green window in bold gold lettering along with two misshapen shamrocks. Inside the place was sparsely and simply furnished. The bar was long and brown and wooden, with around a dozen round barstools in front of it and the perpetual brass foot rail running the length of it. There were four or five tables off to one side— round brown tables that had been in McSwiney's since the saloon opened around the turn of the century. Old men in shabby brown jackets and threadbare trousers sat at the tables with mugs of ale in front of them. A few more men sat silently at the bar. The latest in a long line of bartenders was wiping glasses with a grey dishcloth that may have been white once, and when I eased myself onto a stool he came over and looked at me.

I ordered a double of Irish with a water chaser. He brought the drink and took my money. I left the change on the bar in front of me while I hefted the heavy shot glass and poured the liquor down my throat. It was strong and smoky and it burned its way to my stomach. I took a small sip of water to lubricate the path of the liquor and let my shoulders slump a little as I relaxed over the bar.

A few stools down two men were arguing over the probable outcome of a coming boxing match. They weren't being noisy about it, just making their points in low, even tones. On my right a longshoreman-type was staring moodily into a mug of ale as if he was trying to decide whether or not to drink it. He decided to and wrapped a huge hand around the mug, draining it in one swallow. Then he stared just as moodily into the empty mug.

I ordered a refill and put it with the first drink. I wanted to get drunk, but a controlled sort of drunk that wouldn't leave me off in a gutter somewhere. I'm not that type of drinker. When I drink I take it easy, working to get just the right sort of edge and hold it as long as I can.

After two more drinks I had the edge I was looking for. I could think clearly now, could remember Elaine without wincing, could realize that I was not going to have her again without shutting my eyes to the realization. But life doesn't stop cold when you break up with a woman. I still had a life, a job, a place in the world. I had to figure out where in hell I was going.

It was obvious that I was going to keep the job. It was a good job, and Jukovsky was right when he said I had a future of sorts with the firm. Not quite as glowing a picture as he painted, but a good solid future ahead of me. Already I was taking in better than five grand a year and doing as good a job as any traffic manager Matterhorn had ever had. In time somebody would leave or die and I'd move up to a better slot, with a bigger office and a more impressive title and a fatter pay envelope.

So that was fine. All I had to do was keep my ear to the ground, my shoulder to the wheel, my nose to the grindstone and my eyes open. It was a hell of a position to work in, but I could manage it.

Forgetting Elaine would take some doing. The first step, of course, was to pay her back for the clothing. I figured she'd spent somewhere in excess of a thousand clams on me in one way or the other, not counting the rent and the food and all that. One thousand would square things as far as I was concerned and I knew the money didn't make the least bit of difference to her one way or the other. But it mattered to me. I didn't want to be in debt to her.

The next step was to find another woman. I didn't know many women in New York, but one gal seemed like an obvious potential playmate. Sara Simmons, the girl with the impressive breasts.

Sara Simmons. Innocent, quiet, meek little Sara Simmons.

Little? What was I thinking about? With a chest like that she could be three feet tall and you still couldn't call her little.

A young Irishman a few stools over began to sing. A few men crowded close to him and listened reverently. He sang in an Irish whiskey tenor, which wasn't surprising because he was Irish and had been drinking whiskey. It wasn't obtrusive in the manner of a jukebox or a television set, just nice soft music that was good to listen to.

He sang:

> *Said Lloyd George to Macpherson, "I give you the sack,*
> *To uphold law and order you haven't the knack.*
> *I'll send over Greenwood, a much stronger man,*
> *And fill up the Green Isle with the bold Black and Tan."*

The melody sounded pretty much like "Sweet Betsy From Pike." Nice music this, and a bit more stirring than Sweet Betsy.

> *So he sent them all over to pillage and loot*
> *And burn down the houses, the inmates to shoot.*
> *"To reconquer Ireland," says he, "is my plan*
> *With Macready and Co. and his bold Black and Tan."*

> *The town of Balbriggan they've burned to the ground*
> *While bullets like hailstones were whizzing around;*
> *And women left homeless by this evil clan.*
> *They've waged war on the children, the bold Black and Tan.*

> *From Dublin to Cork and from Thurles to Mayo*
> *Lies a trail of destruction wherever they go;*
> *With England to help and fierce passions to fan,*
> *She must feel bloody proud of her bold Black and Tan.*

Ah, then not by the terrors of England's foul horde,
For ne'er could a nation be ruled by the sword;
For our country we'll have yet in spite of her plan
Or ten times the number of bold Black and Tan.

And, finally:

We defeated Conscription in spite of their threats,
And we're going to defeat old Lloyd George and his pets;
For Ireland and Freedom we're here to a man,
And we'll cut off the balls of the bold Black and Tan.

The tenor kept singing on into the night. He sang "Molly Malone" and "Dark Bosaleen" and "The Shan Van Vocht" and "Skibberdeen" and other songs that I didn't know or don't remember. Some of the others would join him from time to time in the chorus, and the singing was the soft and gentle singing of old men rather than the clamor and boisterousness of a rathskellar. It made good listening.

I had another drink and a few more to keep it company. I sat by myself and I didn't bother anybody and nobody bothered me. When the bartender bought me one on the house I bought one back, but I avoided getting into a conversation with anybody. I wasn't in much of a conversational mood at the time.

Mark Taggert, sitting and drinking alone in an Irish bar on Amsterdam. Sitting and planning to forget a woman named Elaine Rice, sitting and planning the elaborate seduction of a girl named Sara Simmons. Mark Taggert, young businessman with a bright future.

I had another drink.

I needed it.

It was almost closing time when I left the bar. McSwiney's closes at two, well ahead of the 4 a.m. New York closing hour. I walked outside and hailed a cab, a little wary of walking home with a load of good whiskey in my gut. It's too easy to get yourself hit over the head, and I didn't particularly want to get hit over the head.

I paid the cabby at the Touraine and walked to the desk. When I have a night on the town I don't stagger or slur my words. I walk very straight and talk very precisely, and you have to know me very well or get close enough to smell my breath before you can tell I've been drinking. I walked up to the desk and got my key from the night man, not bothering to waste any time talking to him.

The elevator was there waiting for me. I pushed the button that would take me to the eighth floor and settled back while the cage rose in exaggerated slow motion. The ride seemed to take forever; then, suddenly, the car stopped at the eighth floor and the door swung open.

I got out.

My key fit in the lock. The door opened. I undressed and hung up the sport jacket, the slacks, the shirt. I stripped down, took an aspirin to minimize the horror of the morning after, brushed my teeth so that my mouth wouldn't taste quite so vile when I woke up, and called the desk to leave a call for eight the next morning.

I got into bed. And, with all that alcohol swimming around in my bloodstream, I was asleep approximately seven seconds after my head hit the pillow.

Chapter 7

Waking up was a little worse than I had expected but not as bad as it might have been. My head didn't exactly ache but it felt a size or so larger than it usually did. I was momentarily glad that I hadn't taken to wearing a hat. A hat probably wouldn't have fit on the head I was carrying on my shoulders.

My mouth tasted like an underground distillery. I gave my teeth a brushing that helped a little bit and took a hell of a shower—first close to the boiling point, then close to absolute zero. The first half of the shower opened up my pores and turned my skin inside out, while the second half closed the pores back up again and shrank my skin to the proper degree of tautness.

When I stepped out of the refrigerator of a shower and toweled my poor skin dry I felt a little more like a man and a little less like something that lives under rotting logs. I got dressed and waited an ungodly length of time for the elevator. Finally it made it to the eighth floor and I made it down to the main floor. There was a brand new clerk on duty. He threw me a smile and I threw him my key and I went out the door and across the street to a lunch counter.

Scrambled eggs and sausages followed a glass of orange juice into my stomach and sat there grumbling audibly. I had four cups of jet black coffee and three cigarettes and after the coffee and cigarettes everything was all right again. The hangover was gone and my step was light and gay. I paid the check and disappeared into the cold clear light of morning in New York.

I walked crosstown to the building where Matterhorn made its home and elevated upstairs. When you live and work in Manhattan you do one hell of a lot of elevating. For that matter, you spend the bulk of your time going from one place to another, and usually in a stuffy conveyor—an elevator, a subway car, a bus, or something equally unsuited to human habitation.

Sara was already in the office when I got there. We made small talk until the mail clerk managed to get the day's orders to us and then we got to work. The cart came around at ten with coffee and doughnuts and we smiled at each other over the coffee break. Then, when the coffee break was through, we took a work break.

So far it was just a usual day. But Sara Simmons had a surprise in store for her. Ha! She thought I was just a boss, but she didn't know the half of it. Ha! She thought I was just a nice friendly guy, but she didn't know the quarter of it.

Ha!

I took a good long look at her while she was typing up a letter. She was wearing a sweater, and when a girl like Sara Simmons wears a sweater she has to know what she is doing. No girl can have breasts like hers without being aware of them. She was damn well aware of them, and she knew damn well what a pale pink sweater would do for them. Especially when the sweater was at least one size too small.

Ha!

For a moment, as I looked at her sweet little face with the serious I'm-typing-a-letter-for-the-boss-Mr.-Taggert look on her face, I found myself feeling a little guilty about the whole thing.

Then I looked at her breasts again.

That banished the guilt feelings. For one thing, I've never been one to let moral considerations get in the way of my own sensual enjoyment of life and all its pleasures. For another, a girl shaped like that and wearing a sweater like that was looking to get boffed whether she knew it or not.

And if Sara Simmons was looking to get boffed, she did not have to look very far.

All she had to do was open her pretty little eyes and look across the office.

At noon it was lunchtime. If I followed the usual pattern I would bid a businesslike goodbye to Sara and elevate back down to the first floor to eat a sandwich and drink a cup of coffee at the luncheonette on the corner. That's the way I had spent my lunch hour every day so far that week, and the weeks before as well.

But that was different.

In those days I had possessed a mistress. And I possessed one no longer. Now I possessed bachelor's quarters in a midtown hotel, and midday celibacy no longer had a place in my life. I was a free man again. If I wanted to take my secretary to lunch, why in the world shouldn't I?

Why indeed?

So I did.

"Sara," I said, "let's go have lunch."

She sort of jumped. Then she looked as though she figured I meant we should each go our separate ways. This was a healthy sign—it meant that the notion of eating together had occurred to her, but she didn't think it would occur to me.

"Come on," I said. "It's about time I bought you a meal."

"Oh," she said.

"There's a nice German restaurant around the corner on 44th. I sort of feel like a decent meal."

She was flustered. She got up from her chair, obviously very happy and also very nervous, and asked me if I would wait while she freshened up. Then she disappeared down the hallway and into the ladies room, taking a good deal less time at it than the average doll. When she came out she looked exactly the same as when she walked in, but this doesn't make any difference to a female. They have to go through the ritual of powdering and unpowdering their noses come hell or high water.

We made more small talk on the way downstairs and along the street to the Blue Boar. A stiff-backed waiter in a powder blue uniform found us a table and took my order for two dry Gibsons. He brought them and we drank them.

The drink loosened her up and she searched through the menu avidly.

"Gee," she bubbled. "There are so many things I never even heard of before. What's good?"

"The sauerbraten's good," I guessed. Since I had never been

to the Blue Boar before it was a calculated guess, based on the knowledge that there wasn't a German restaurant in New York where the sauerbraten was less than good. It's pretty tough to do a bad job on sauerbraten.

"What's that?"

"Haven't you ever had it before?"

She shook her head.

"Ever have pot roast?"

"Sure."

"It's pot roast," I said. "Sweet-and-sour pot roast with red cabbage and potato dumpling."

"It sounds good."

"It is good."

"Is that what you're having?"

I nodded, and she decided she would have some too. I think if I had told her I was having chicken farts on toasted rye-krisp she would have ordered the same just to keep me company.

I gave the waiter our order and stared at her breasts until the food came. We babbled about superficial things, and even with the superficial babble I found out that she was a lot deeper and more intelligent than I had figured at first. Hustead-cum-Trundleberg doesn't generally make for a stimulating personality or a beautifully shining intellect, but Sara had a good little mind and a lot of feeling for people. She was fun to be with, and I was enjoying myself. But just as the conversation started to get rolling I would get another look at those breasts, those stupendous, fantastic breasts, whereupon my tongue would get in the way of my eye teeth until I couldn't see what I was saying.

The waiter reappeared, back still unbent. He brought our food and proved me right—the sauerbraten was the end of the world, the potato dumpling properly luscious, the cabbage more than palatable. We quieted down somewhat in order to empty our plates.

We passed up the dessert with an effort and I tackled coffee and a cigarette while she put away a glass of milk. Nice wholesome girl, Sara Simmons. Drinking milk at the end of the meal. I wondered if she needed it to fill up those two little milk-factories of hers.

"We'd better be getting back to the office," she said when it was time for us to be getting back to the office.

"I suppose so. No need to rush—we'll finish ahead of time anyway."

She nodded, but I don't think she even heard what I was saying. She was staring at me adoringly with those big brown eyes and I had a good feeling that Sara Simmons was just a few steps away from a conquest. The standard operating procedure called for me to half-ignore her for a day or two, then take her out for a heavy dinner date and try like hell to wind up in her pants before the night was over. But the look she was giving me made me decide to live dangerously and push my luck.

"Sara," I said, "will you have dinner with me tonight?"

She stared.

I decided to try the all-alone-in-the-big-city approach. I smiled and lowered my voice.

"I don't want to rush you," I told her. "You may think that you have to accept because I'm your boss, but I don't want you to feel that way. It's just that . . . well, living alone and spending all my time alone can get pretty . . . well, lonely. And I thought maybe if you didn't have anything planned we might get together."

"I don't have anything planned."

"Then how about it? We'll make a night of it—have a good dinner, maybe take in a show. You're a very lovely girl and besides—" here I turned on all the famous Mark Taggert charm "—you're awfully nice company, Sara."

The look in her eyes told me I had it made.

And then she said: "I don't think I can have dinner with you tonight, Mark."

When I got up off the floor I started to ask her why in the world not. But she cut me off.

"But *you* can have dinner with *me*, if you'd like. You see, I have a couple of steaks I took out of the freezer this morning and I wouldn't want them to spoil. But if you'd like to come over and let me cook them for us—"

"I'd love to."

I was in.

Like Flynn.

The rest of the day dragged. This wasn't surprising, because after a girl like Sara Simmons invites you to her apartment for dinner almost anything seems anticlimactic. A day of bills of lading is number one in the department of anticlimaxes anyhow, and it was right at the top of the dull list that afternoon. I suffered through it, rewarded at one point by a special word of praise from

Jukovsky, who hinted that managing traffic might seem a little unchallenging to a guy like me, and that there might be something more inspiring in the offing and not too long. This was fine with me, and I beamed appreciatively when he told me.

Sara lived alone, which made things just that much better. She had this apartment on Bank Street on the west side of Greenwich Village which she had been sharing with a theatrical hopeful who also hailed from Ohio, but she was living alone now because the theatrical hopeful had taken up with an assistant director, apparently in a last-ditch effort to break into off-Broadway theatre. This, I decided, was encouraging—a taste of Village life combined with the roommate's sexual precocity was a sign that Sara had no doubt been around a bit. All of which seemed to indicate a relatively easy trip to the bedroom and a lot of staying power between the sheets.

We took a cab to her apartment—I was taking a hell of a lot of cabs these days—and walked up two flights of stairs to her place. The building was nicer than a lot of the roach-traps in the Village and her apartment was furnished cheaply but in good taste. I relaxed into a comfortable chair after she turned down my offer to help with the steaks. Then, to the accompaniment of delicious cooking smells from the kitchen, I buried myself in a paperback novel.

By the time I dug myself back out of the paperback novel dinner was ready. She knew how to cook steak—thick and tender and bloody rare. And she knew how to serve it. No potatoes or vegetables cluttering up the plate, just good rare meat all alone by itself. It was a delight just to look at it.

Then she disappeared again just as I was picking up my knife and fork. She came back with a bottle and a corkscrew and handed them to me.

"Here," she said. "Can you open this?"

The wine was Beaujolais, a good red Burgundy. I fooled around with the corkscrew until I managed to get the damned cork out and filled our glasses with the wine.

We didn't talk during dinner. Anybody who wastes his time talking when he has a hunk of steak in front of him and a glass of wine at his elbow has nothing wrong with him that a first-class prefrontal lobotomy wouldn't cure. We ate, and I refilled our glasses with more of the wine, and we ate some more.

The steak was finished before the wine was. I filled our glasses and carried mine to the small two-passenger sofa, a coy little maneuver designed to make her come and sit next to me.

It worked.

When I turned to her there was no need to play games any more. Her eyes were shining and her lips were parted and she was a woman waiting to be kissed.

So I did the obvious thing.

I kissed her.

Her mouth was warm and tasted of wine. She came against me like a hungry kitten and her hands were cool as frozen silk on the back of my neck. She gave me her mouth and my tongue tasted the sweetness of it, licking the poignant taste of wine from her lips.

As if by a prearranged signal we stood up and walked from the room. She sagged against me and her hip brushed mine as we walked. I couldn't help staring at her body, that beautiful body that was going to be mine in a matter of minutes. She was so beautiful, so young and fresh and vibrant. And when she kissed it was perfume and honey and the compelling and delicious taste of wine.

We embraced in the bedroom. We could hardly stay on our feet and we held each other for support, clutching one another close.

Then we parted and she pulled her sweater over her head and I couldn't believe that the flimsy black bra could hold what was in it. Then her skirt was off and I saw that her thighs were beautiful—twin alabaster columns that rose from neat feet and ankles to rounded, swelling thighs.

Her arms went behind her back and the bra nearly broke with the motion. Then it was off and I saw her breasts, and they were without any shadow of doubt the most perfect breasts in the entire world. White and unblemished, huge and firm and swelling, with the red nipples all hard and glowing from her sexual excitement.

"Take me, Mark. Love me."

Everything I did served to heighten our passion. I kissed her and the pair of us were on fire.

"Mark, don't wait!"

I wanted to wait.

I wanted to prolong it, to make it take as long as it possibly could. I wanted to build to an agony that was more beautiful than anything else in the world. I wanted to drive our passion higher and higher until it exploded.

But I couldn't wait.

I couldn't wait another minute.

And then I got the shock of my life.

Sara Simmons was a virgin.

CHAPTER 8

"You should have told me," I said.

"I was afraid to."

"What do you mean?"

"I was afraid you wouldn't want me. If you knew I was a virgin I thought you might not want to make love to me."

"That's silly."

"Is it?"

"Of course."

"You still would have wanted me?"

"Certainly."

"I'm glad," she said. "But I didn't know and I didn't want to take any chances. I wanted you so much, Mark. So I tried to act like a real woman of the world and pretend I had oodles of experience."

I grinned. "You put on one hell of a good act."

"I did?"

"Uh-huh. You had me fooled."

Her smile grew wider. "I really didn't know what I was doing, Mark. I had to sort of play it by ear."

"You weren't faking, were you?"

"You mean when I acted excited?"

"Yeah."

Her mouth went solemn. "I wasn't faking at all," she said. "I couldn't fake something like that. I was so excited I could hardly breathe."

I kissed her again. "You should have told me," I said again. "I would have been more gentle with you."

"It doesn't matter."

I moved away from her so that I could look at her, at all of her from head to toe. She didn't shrink under my gaze the way so many women do. She was proud of her body, proud of being a woman and pleased to have me look at her with raw admiration in my eyes.

She was beautiful.

I told her so.

"Do you really think so?"

"Uh-huh."

"Do you like my body?"

I told her what I thought of her body.

"Do you . . . like my breasts?"

"Any man who doesn't like your breasts is obviously homosexual."

"But they're so big!"

"That's one of the things I like."

"Honestly?"

"Honestly."

She put her hands on her breasts and looked down at them intently. "I used to hate them," she said. "I used to hate the sight of them. They made me feel positively abnormal."

"You *are* abnormal. You're far superior to normal."

"I really used to hate them," she went on. "When I walk into a room I always feel as though I'm just following my breasts inside."

I had to laugh at that.

"They've been this size since I was fourteen," she said, "They started to grow when I was in the sixth grade and they kept right on growing. I used to get so darned embarrassed the way the boys would stare at me in class."

"I don't blame them."

"Mark, do you honestly like them?"

"I love them," I assured her. "The more I look at them the more I love them."

"I'm glad."

"What I can't understand," I said, "is how in the world you managed to stay a virgin with a shape like yours."

"In Hustead?" She wrinkled up her nose when she said the name of the town, as if even the name had an unpleasant smell to it.

"Even in Hustead."

"It wasn't hard."

"I don't see how the boys let you alone."

"They didn't," she told me. "I just didn't let them do anything. I didn't go out and neck and pet the way other girls at school did. I just wasn't interested."

"What about Trundleberg?"

For a long moment she didn't say anything. A strange sad light came into her eyes and I was afraid that I had asked the wrong question.

"There was a boy at Trundleberg," she said.

I waited for her to go on.

"I . . . I was in love with him, Mark."

Her eyes were misty. I reached out a hand to touch her, to comfort her.

"He was in love with me, too. I was a sophomore and he was a senior and we were very much in love. He wanted to make love to me but we were going to be married and I made him wait because . . . well, I guess I was afraid, more than anything else. I thought it would be better to wait, too."

She looked away. "So we waited."

She paused again, and this time when she spoke her voice was thin and drawn. "We shouldn't have waited, Mark. While we were waiting, Ted—his name was Ted—well, he died, Mark. He died."

I didn't say anything. There was nothing to say.

"A plane crash," she went on. "He lived in St. Louis and he was flying home for Christmas vacation. The plane just blew up in the middle of the air and that was the end. Period, finished. The end."

"Those things happen."

"Of course they do, and I'm over it now. But I'll always be sorry that I didn't at least make love with him first. We should have made love, Mark. It would have been right and there wasn't any point to waiting. We loved each other and we wanted each other and I was just being a baby about the whole thing. I should have let him."

She took a deep breath. For awhile she had been on the verge of tears but now she had a firm grip on herself and I knew she was going to be all right.

"So I decided not to wait any more," she continued. "I didn't do anything at Trundleberg because there wasn't anybody I wanted. And there hadn't been anybody until I met you in the office. But once I met you and wanted you and saw that you wanted me I was through with waiting."

"Are you glad we made love?"

"Very glad, Mark."

"I'm sorry I hurt you."

"But I enjoyed it," she said. "It . . . it was something very wonderful."

I looked at her again. She was my woman now and she was so beautiful I felt the hunger building within me again. I wanted her, wanted her very much.

I kissed her.

"It will be better this time," I told her, reaching for her. "It will be better for you. I'm going to make it good for you, darling. You're going to love it."

I was right.

She really was a wonderful girl—a fine, sweet, human and sensitive person. A most rare type of individual who was fun in bed and fun out of bed, efficient in the office and unbeatable in the bedroom. Bright and youthful, clever and companionable, sweet and lovable.

We didn't live together. It might have been nice, but there were just too many objections to an arrangement of that nature. Business and pleasure were fun to mix but it's easy to louse up both ends if you scramble them too thoroughly. We didn't want that to happen. I was still the boss and she was still my secretary, and by a mutual unspoken agreement we kept the business side of our relationship on a simple business level. I dictated letters and issued memos and she typed letters and opened mail and performed the other trivia which secretaries perform. It was sensible, and it got the work done.

I kept my room at the Touraine and settled down there. I opened a checking account at a Fifth Avenue bank in the forties, found a guy on the block who did my laundry and dry cleaning, settled on one particular coffee shop for breakfast and one particular restaurant for lunch. Bit by bit I was settling into a regular routine, and it was the first chance I'd had to put down genuine roots in several years.

It was pleasant. When a routine becomes comfortable it loses the appearance of a rut. The Organization Man life had seemed horrible, but the life I had wasn't the Organization Man's life by any means. My job wasn't the cut-and-dried nonsense, and Marty Jukovsky believed in hiring men who would be more interested in a fat paycheck than in pension plans and stock-purchase deals that attracted the idiots who were so worried about security that they wound up living the secure and purposeless life of a goldfish.

The hotel was pleasant, especially after I invested in a cheap but serviceable portable record player and a stack of LPs. A few prints on the walls livened the place and made it look a little less like a hotel room and a little more like a home. Then, when I crawled into bed and tossed a stack of records on the record player and closed my eyes and drifted off to sleep listening to the music, I was as happy as I would have been almost anywhere else.

Sara and I were spending a great deal of time together. At the same time, however, we didn't monopolize each other. She was doing a lot of reading as well as thinking about taking a Master's at NYU in a year or so and thus needed plenty of time to herself. And I wasn't demanding—I wanted time alone, too, time to relax and roam around the city, time to read and time to think.

In the office I was the boss and she was the secretary. After hours we either went our separate ways—which was the case at least two nights of the week—or I took her out for a dinner, or we went to her apartment and worked our way through a pair of steaks. When I took her out I picked up the tab; when we went to her place she bought the food and wine. That was the way she wanted it and I didn't try to argue with her.

On weekends we spent most of our time together, and it was only on weekends that I would sleep over at her apartment. Other times I dressed and went back to my hotel after we had finished with our love making, but on weekends we permitted ourselves full nights together. We would get a little bit high on wine and crawl into bed, ready to perform new and wonderful feats between the sheets.

During those weeks I also got started on the complex project of repaying Elaine. Every Friday Marty handed me my paycheck;

every Friday I mailed a check to Elaine. I was sending her twenty-five dollars a week—at which I rate I figured I'd be able to repay her in something resembling forty weeks—until suddenly I was able to send her fifty bucks instead.

The reason for this was relatively simple.

Marty raised me to one-and-a-half yards per.

I was calling him Marty by this time. I had decided that traffic managing, simple and interesting though it may be, was not quite enough for an industrious soul like Mark Taggert. And it wasn't just vaulting ambition overleaping its goal. Strange as it may seem, I was getting fairly interested in the affairs of Matterhorn Press. I wanted to get some idea what the hell happened outside of the traffic department, figuring logically that this would not only give me a chance to be in line for a promotion but would also help me be a better traffic manager.

I started out by staying late those evenings when Sara and I didn't have anything doing. I got a pass from Marty and meandered around the building inspecting files. It wasn't the easiest way to get the hang of a business, but a careful study of everything from promotional material and opening sales letters to balance sheets and correspondence with authors gave me a fairly good insight into the *modus operandi* of Matterhorn Press. When you read thick files of correspondence you have to be a complete and total clod not to pick up something. Besides, I like to read other people's mail.

The self-improvement campaign was going great guns, but after a few weeks I was running out of files to read and it seemed sensible to find a more orderly and systematic way to get the necessary understanding of Matterhorn's operations.

So I went to Marty.

He was more than pleased. He was thrilled, and he told me so. His wide little eyes got a faraway look in them and he smiled at me like a father. When I told him how I had been reading through files, just tossing the information in as though it was something insignificant, he was properly impressed. And he was more than cooperative—he not only told me what to look at and what to read, but set things up so that the two of us would stay late a couple evenings a week and he would explain things to me.

This was fine with me. It was also fine with him, and he decided the extra couple of nights merited an extra twenty-five a week, which was also fine with me.

It didn't take any genius to figure out that I was being groomed for something bigger than the silly slot of traffic manager. I don't know how big, but I knew I was due for a step up the old ladder in the near future.

Then Marty told me what the step was.

"Mark," he said one Tuesday night as we sat at our desks gobbling ham-and-swiss-on-rye from the delicatessen down the street, "you've been doing a lot of work lately."

"Just my job."

He polished off his sandwich and took a gulp of beer from the can. "More than your job. Hell, I saw the letter you wrote last week to the schoolboard in Madison, Wisconsin. You were trying to talk those guys into ordering our whole set of arithmetic texts."

This had been a pet project of mine. I always tried to turn

routine letters or gripe-answers into letters that were vaguely personal as well as businesslike, and when some clod in Madison made some noise to me about how rough things were with three different arithmetic systems in operation in his school system, I sympathized like a nice boy and promptly recommended our line.

"Mark," Marty went on, "you don't know what you were asking from the poor slob. Madison would have to order eight grades' worth of books in order to change over. That would mean junking god knows how many texts, some of them purchased within the last couple years."

"I'm sorry if I went out of the way, Marty. I thought I'd give us a plug. That's all."

"That's all?"

"Sure, I—"

"I got a letter from the superintendent of schools," he cut in. "Today."

"Yeah? What did he say?"

"They're taking your advice."

"You mean . . ."

"I mean they'll be buying all their math texts from us. They're making a complete switch, and the guy was so pleased with the personal interest you were taking in his problems that we'll be supplying every textbook used in the city of Madison in a year or two. This guy likes you, Mark."

I sort of stammered.

"I like you, too." He beamed at me. "You've got the right touch. And you've got the interests of both the company and the customer at heart. That's important, Mark. A guy who just looks out for himself or his company doesn't last too long in this business. Textbooks is a field where you have to maintain good relations with the guys who do the buying, and they can tell when you just think of them as someone who pays the rent on the office."

He finished his beer and stuck a cigar in his mouth. He bit off the end, spat it halfway across the room, and set the end of the cigar on fire with a wooden match. Thick smoke billowed across at me.

"You're too good to stay in traffic," he went on. "But you've been turning into something of a problem. There's no other department where I can stick you and nobody I want to kick out. I didn't know what the hell to do with you."

"Well—"

"Hang on," he said. "I finally figured it out. If I can't push anybody out, I'll just have to stick you on top of the rest of them. Know what I'm talking about?"

I had an idea.

"I want you where you won't be buried in any cubbyhole," he said. "Some spot where you can be right under me with your nose in every last facet of this company's operations.

"Mark, I have a feeling this place is going to be needing a General Manager. What do you think?"

CHAPTER 9

Horatio Alger had nothing on me. I had it made, when you come right down to it. Made in the shade. The world was in my back pocket and I was in the pleasant process of buttoning down the flap.

General Manager.

General Manager of Matterhorn Press.

Now this was one hell of an impressive title. *Traffic Manager* might almost move some people to gulps of admiration, but I knew better. *General Manager* was something entirely different.

Something pleasant to contemplate.

I said it over to myself. *General Manager*, I said.

Mark Taggert, General Manager.

General Manager—Mark Taggert.

It sounded good.

Marty explained what the job entailed. I would be second in command, handling top-level stuff for every department and working directly with Marty on a good many things. We kicked it around for awhile and I was surprised to realize I had some fairly decent ideas on a whole lot of Matterhorn business, ranging from a sketchy notion for a top-drawer promotion campaign of our college lit line to a whole slew of typographical ideas for the production department. The job would not only be a golden opportunity but a hell of a challenge as well, and I could see myself getting a lot of kicks out of the whole business.

And out of the salary.

Twelve big bills a year to start, Marty said. And, while the salary would never go much higher than fifteen grand—which is high enough, damn it—he'd be paying me off in stock bonuses as time went by. After we ended the conversation for the evening I hauled out a pencil and paper and privately figured out that I'd own a third of the company within fifteen years.

This was attractive.

Damned attractive.

Yeah.

I celebrated that night, a happy celebration even if it was a solo affair. I had myself a late steak dinner at a restaurant that serves nothing but steak, with a few stiff drinks before and a pony of brandy afterwards. I ate slowly and enjoyed it; then I went to a nightclub on 52nd Street for the rest of the evening.

The strip clubs on 52nd Street are a waste of time, but my main object for the evening was to waste time and money. I couldn't see Sara—she was busy—so I figured the next best thing was to get quietly fried while I watched pretty girls take off their clothes. There is something about watching a pretty girl take off her clothes that is awfully nice. While it's not quite the same as giving her a hand with them, it is still a good way to give your eyes something delicious to look at. Any man who stops watching ought to be buried at least six feet deep and promptly forgotten. Brother, when you don't look, you're dead.

The 52nd Street traps are the joints with broken-down doormen standing outside roping the tourists in and looking for all the world like the jerks who herd tourists onto busses for a trip to Chinatown. The liquor is vile and costs better than a buck a shot, the minimum is high and before you know it you've spent all your money. Two classes of people frequent the clubs—tourists who don't know better and jokers on expense accounts who don't really care how much an evening costs.

I was in a third class, a brand new category. I knew better, I wasn't on an expense account, and I just plain didn't care.

So there.

A ten-spot bought a table in front from the headwaiter. A waiter took my order and brought me a drink that tasted as though someone had drank it before me and now it was back for a second try.

But I didn't really care.

What I came to see was busy on stage, and I was having a high old time just doing nothing and watching her. She had the improbable name of Nudi Flesh, which meant her mother probably knew her as Hermione Byessovtroski. I didn't care what the hell anybody called her.

She was fun to watch.

She had this mane of bright red hair that was the best money could buy and lots of white ivory skin. She came on wearing this peekaboo type thing about the same color as her hair, and it set me wondering whether she bought the peekaboo thing to match her hair or bought the hair to match the peekaboo thing. I decided that it didn't really make much difference one way or the other, but it was something to think about.

This Mickey Mouse band they had was making horrible music and Nudi was sort of dancing to it. I say *sort of* because the girl had two left feet that she kept stepping on. Fortunately such aesthetic considerations were comparatively unimportant.

Nobody was looking at her feet.

She got rid of the peekaboo type thing, you see, and what was under it was primarily Nudi.

Then, suddenly, there was no G-string.

At least not one that you could see. There was this flesh-colored affair, of course, and you could only tell it was there because of what you *didn't* see, not because you could see the thing.

Then, after she danced around some more, she suddenly went into what I guess was her specialty.

She spread her legs a few feet apart, you see, and she put her hands on her hips, you see, and then she bent way forward and began shaking her chest from one side to the other, an excruciating grin on her pretty little paper-doll face.

And the breasts danced.

You've got to picture this in your mind. Here's this big creamy redhead, you understand, and all you see of her is two nice legs and an equally nice fanny. Between these legs a pair of large breasts is rolling back and forth in time to lousy music. Below the breasts is an upside-down head with a mass of red hair brushing the dust off the stage.

Yeah.

It was fun, in a gruesome sort of a way. For awhile I couldn't quite understand the appeal of the whole thing. Then it began to reach me.

Yeah.

Nudi finished, finally. The morons applauded and she came back and blew kisses around the room. Then she disappeared.

The emcee who followed her told dirty jokes that Washington almost fell into the Delaware laughing over. The comic who followed him told jokes that made their original appearance in Latin. Then this other chick came out and did a relatively straight strip. She was fairly attractive in a long-stemmed sort of way but she didn't do much to me.

Meanwhile a broken-down blonde was trying to take my picture for a dollar and her broken-down contemporary was trying to take something else for ten times as much. She pulled up a chair without an invitation, coaxed me into buying her a drink of vodka-flavored water, and without further ado suggested we go to her place and lighten my wallet.

She was very upset when I told her to disappear. She tried to convince me of just what I was missing, describing the whole affair in the most glowing and graphic terms imaginable.

I didn't want to disappoint her.

But I wanted even less to crawl into bed with her.

So she disappeared, her feathers ruffled and her self-confidence wilted like a camellia in a steam bath. Then Nudi wound up on the stage again and started to go into her act. It was time for me to go, but Nudi was sort of fun to watch and I was high enough so that the taste of the liquor I was drinking didn't seem to irritate me any more.

She did the same bit again. Her flimsy garments were an off-blue this time, and I mused over the thought that she might have dyed her hair blue to match. She should have, dammit. The gal was short on imagination.

By the time she had that red hair brushing the floor and those breasts shaking like a hammock in a hurricane something very deep and profound occurred to me. I suddenly realized a most important and subtle point of fact.

Right then, at that particular moment, I could be sleeping with a better-looking woman than the one I was staring at so avidly.

And the hell of it was, the first woman who came to mind was Elaine Rice.

You know, for an alcoholic moment I actually toyed with the idea of running over to that Park Avenue palace and trying to throw Elaine for a fall.

I started thinking about her, wondering what in the world she might be doing. By now she had probably taken up with another guy. That was the natural thing for a healthy, passionate woman like her to do—and I couldn't understand why the thought annoyed me.

But it did.

Whatever she was doing, I decided, there was no place for me in her life or her in mine. Sure, I could go over there and try for a quick one. In all probability I'd get thrown out on my ear and deserve it. But if I didn't, if I managed to get her on her back, all I would succeed in doing would be to louse the two of us up again. And that was something I didn't want to do.

Sara though—Sara would be home. And Sara would not throw me out on my ear, and with Sara there would be no chance of anybody getting all balled up. Theoretically we were supposed to spend the night apart, but a quick glance at my watch revealed the happy news that it was after midnight.

So I paid a ridiculous check which still didn't bother me in the least, left a high tip for the rotten service I had been treated to, and got the hell out of the club with nary a backward glance at the still-swinging breasts of Nudi Flesh. Let her swing 'em until they fell off. I didn't care. I had a better pair of breasts to fool around with.

I hailed a cab and gave the cabby Sara's address.

I got out of the cab in front of Sara's building. I walked up the steps and into the vestibule and leaned heavily on her buzzer, hoping she hadn't gone to sleep. Her apartment was in the rear and I couldn't tell if she was up without ringing.

She buzzed back right away. I pulled open the door and climbed steps, counting them diligently to myself. There were fourteen of them.

I knocked on the door.

"Who's there?"

"Me—Mark."

She opened the door.

She was a vision. A black nightgown more peekabooish than Nudi Flesh's outfit was covering her, and there was nothing under it but Sara Simmons, of which there was just the right amount. Her eyes were shining and I knew she was glad to see me.

"I'm glad to see you," she said.

"Did I wake you?"

She shook her head. "I couldn't sleep. I'm glad you came, Mark. I was sort of hoping you would come but I didn't expect you."

"I got lonesome."

"I'm glad."

I put my hands on her shoulders and gave her a little kiss. Her lips were warm and I knew that she wanted me as much as I wanted her, which was saying a hell of a lot.

I slipped an arm around her waist and she leaned against it. Her flesh through the nightie was cool and soft. We started walking toward the bedroom automatically, two minds with but a single thought, two bodies with but a single objective. Halfway to the bedroom door I stopped abruptly and kissed the side of her neck. She caught her breath and I knew how passionate she was then, how perfect a night it was for me to have come.

Chapter 10

Much later I remembered that there was something I had wanted to tell her. I thought a minute. What was it?

Ah, yes. The promotion.

"Sara," I began, "how would you like to be the secretary of the general manager of Matterhorn Press?"

"Do you mean I'm being fired? You want to kick me out and have me work for somebody else?"

"No—just thought you might like a promotion."

"What do I need with a promotion?"

"I don't know."

"Well," she said, "to hell with the general manager. I'll stick with the traffic manager, if it's all right with you."

"Sara," I said, feeling a little sorry for the poor bewildered thing, "I want you to be my secretary."

"Thank God for that."

"But I also want you to be the secretary of the new general manager. He'll be having a tough job anyway and he deserves the best secretary in the business."

"Wait a second," she said. "Who is this guy that you care so much who his secretary is?"

"His name is Mark Taggert."

"Huh?"

She was spinning in circles by now so I pushed her back down on the bed and kissed her and then explained the whole bit from start to finish. She stayed quiet while I told her, anxious to get the story straight once and for all. I started with the staying late and reading the files project and led up to the conversations with Marty and the bomb he dropped in my lap a few hours ago.

By the time I finished her eyes were shining.

"Mark," she said. "Oh, Mark!"

"It's a pretty good deal."

"Good? It's wonderful. I'm tremendously happy for you."

"You mean you're willing to be the secretary of the general manager now?"

"Ready and willing."

"That's good."

I put my head on the pillow next to hers and we looked into each other's eyes. She moved her face closer to mine and gave me a shy little kiss on the cheek. Then she draped one arm around me and rubbed the small of my back.

"This calls for a celebration, Mark."

"What does?"

"Your promotion, silly. We have to celebrate the fact that my man is about to become General Manager of Matterhorn Press."

"We just did."

"Just did what?"

"Just celebrated," I explained patiently. "What the hell do you think we were doing a little while ago?"

"I thought we were—"

"Yeah. What kind of a celebration did you have in mind, anyway?"

Her eyes twinkled. "Guess."

"Again?"

"Why not?"

Afterwards I was too tired to sleep.

Sara was justifiably exhausted. I waited until she was sleeping soundly and slipped out of bed. There was a beat-up bathrobe in her closet that I kept for such occasions and I put it on. I closed the bedroom door behind me and blew a kiss in her direction.

There was a pot of coffee on the stove and I turned on the gas beneath it. I located a cup and a saucer in the cupboard and set a place for myself. The coffee heated up and I poured myself a cup, sitting down with it at the kitchen table. It was hot and strong and properly bitter, and with a cigarette for company it tasted wonderful.

For some reason I was pretty mixed up. I had the world in my back pocket, sure. All I had to do was button down the flap.

Sure.

So here I was, Mark Taggert, ex-bum and ex-drifter and about-to-be General Manager of Matterhorn Press.

With the world in my back pocket.

But what the hell was I going to do with it?

I closed my eyes and pictured myself in twenty years. I'd be half-bald by then, probably, with a little paunch from too much good living. I'd be a little old for as much horsing around but still in condition to go a few every now and then.

But how would I keep from going crazy? What the hell would I do with myself?

The truth was a long time coming. I was half-done with the second cup of coffee and matching cigarette before I had everything straightened out in my head. Once the answer came to me I laughed, tossed my head nervously and tried to get the idea out of my mind.

It wouldn't go away.

I had everything I needed—except one thing. I had all the factors of a perfect life, a magically ideal existence, except for one.

Just one.

A wife.

The first time I got the notion I laughed, and I told myself quite firmly that I needed a wife like a belly dancer needed a girdle. Marriage—who needs it? Who wants to be tied down to one woman forever, to have a house somewhere instead of an apartment, a mortgage to pay and expenses all over the place? Who wants a houseful of kids getting in the way all the time, walking into your bedroom while you're trying to make love to their mother, growing out of their clothes and asking stupid questions all the time that you don't know the answer to?

Who needs it?

Well, I needed it, wise guy. I needed it very much, because without all that paraphernalia I might as well be on the bum again with no job and no apartment and no suits and jackets and no woman named Sara Simmons and no bank account and no future and nothing in the world but a laundry bag to keep me company. I needed it, and I needed it for a set of very good reasons.

You can go only so far alone. You can go fairly far that way, and there's a little truth in the proverb which states that he travels fastest who travels alone. You go very fast that way.

But you don't get any place worth going.

Now I appreciated an aspect of legal marriage that hadn't appealed to me before. It was a much more permanent thing than a shack-up could possibly be. Hell, I've known people who've just plain lived together for years without a wedding, but the average couple doesn't stay together too long unless the gal has a ring on her finger.

And I wanted permanence.

I also wanted that houseful of kids I was talking about in such uncomplimentary terms a minute or two ago. I sat there, believe it or not, and I started to think of first names that go well with Taggert.

Did you ever see this cartoon: There's a little kid, a smart-looking little kid, and there's this guidance teacher type sitting behind a desk with a pipe in his mouth, saying very patiently: "Arnold, it's not enough to be a genius. You have to be a genius at something."

I all at once knew how poor little Arnold felt. It wasn't enough to get married—you had to marry someone.

Sara, of course.

So it was settled, except for asking her. Which, I decided, was the same as saying that it was settled. Sara would want to marry me as much as I wanted to marry her, and in a month or so we would be Mr. and Mrs. Mark Taggert, and in a month or so after that we would have our own home in one of the better suburbs, and in nine or ten months after that we would be hatching a child.

I wondered what it would be like to be married to Sara, to have her beside me whenever I woke up, to have that girl belong to me and to no one else in the world. I had been first with her; now no one else would ever get a chance to sample what I had discovered.

And, damn it, I would probably wind up being faithful to her. She had enough downright sexiness to her so that I wouldn't have to chase other women. I always had a strong feeling that the men who have to cheat on their wives were men who had never grown up. Just having Sara would be enough for me; I was pretty sure of it.

Even for a slob like me who has never spent more than an hour and a half on a decision in his life, getting married was sort of a jarring notion. I was all for it by now, but it still had me shaking a little.

I didn't propose over breakfast. I suppose it's possible to propose at the conclusion of a plate of scrambled eggs, but somehow my aesthetic sense rebelled at the notion. I kept my plan to myself and contented myself with smiling secretively at Sara.

We went to the office together. I tackled the morning mail and dictated several letters; then the pleasant interlude of the coffee break was upon us. I sat at my desk with a cup of coffee and a cruller that had seen better days, still not tired even though I hadn't had any sleep all night. I looked at her, and I decided that she looked very beautiful, and that a coffee break was as good a time to propose as any.

She looked up at me. I walked over to her and sat down on the edge of her desk, my face serious.

"Sara," I said, "I have something to ask you."

She waited.

"Sara, I . . . will you marry me?"

I waited for her to say yes. The question didn't seem to have come as much of a shock to her as I had expected. She took it all very calmly, and she looked into my eyes with understanding and affection shining in her own eyes.

She said: "No, Mark. I won't marry you."

Chapter 11

"You heard right, Mark. I don't want to marry you."

I let that sink in. "Okay," I said. "Explain."

Her eyes were very serious, her voice level and almost totally lacking in emotion when she spoke. I listened to her very carefully.

"Two reasons," she said. "The first is the most important one, I guess, so I'll tell you that one first. I don't love you, Mark."

That line sort of slugged me between the eyes. "But—"

"But I sleep with you—is that what you were going to say?"

"That's not what I was going to say, but I suppose it'll do for a starter."

She took a deep breath and let it out slowly. "I sleep with you," she said, "because I happen to enjoy sleeping with you. I enjoy it very much. I've decided that you don't have to be in love with a person to make love with him. I went too long without satisfying certain physical and emotional needs, Mark, and I don't want to lead a chaste little-girl life until I meet the right man. If sleeping with you without being in love with you lowers me in your esteem, I'm very sorry."

"You know it doesn't."

"I know." She lowered her eyes for a moment and looked at the top of her desk. I watched her very carefully and looked deep into her eyes when she raised them to meet mine again.

"Sara," I said, "I think you've got a few things wrong. You can't tell me you sleep with me only because we can make it physically. You must feel something or else there's nothing more to it than plain sex. I can't believe that. What we have is something a lot deeper than that."

"Of course it is. I'm afraid I phrased things badly at the beginning. I didn't mean that I didn't love you."

"What—"

"Let me finish. I *love* you, Mark. I love you very much, and I know that I probably always will love you. But I'm not *in love* with you. Do you see what I'm getting at?"

"Frankly," I said, "no."

"Let me try it this way," she said finally. "I love you in that I feel very close to you, that I care a great deal about you. When something good happens for you I'm very happy. When you're down in the dumps it drags me down. I share your moods and I enjoy being with you and not just in a sexual sense."

That was gratifying, let me tell you.

"But I'm not in love with you. There's a difference between loving a person and being in love with him. You can love many persons, feeling for them and sympathizing with them and being close to them—and even sleeping with them, for that matter.

But *in love* is a state that is very different. It means that this one person—and only one person at a time, and not too many people during your whole lifetime—this one person is the most important person in the world. It doesn't mean that you can't live without that person, but it means that life would be a tremendous amount less bearable without him and—"

She broke off. I knew what she was driving at but I had to let her say it all.

"It's a matter of degree, I suppose. I think *in love* is just a type of love that is so much stronger than anything else that it turns the rest of the world upside-down. But I do know this: I'm not going to settle for anything less than the top. I'll sleep with anybody I want to sleep with, Mark, but I won't marry him unless I'm in love with him."

I said: "I see." And, strangely, I did. I saw not only that I had been handed my hat but that she had good reason to hand it to me. My reactions were hard to pin down just then. I didn't make any outward show of emotions, and inside I was pretty mixed up—justifiably so, I might add. I didn't have a tremendous flood of disappointment or anger or even of loss, which should have been natural. I had, inescapably the feeling of rejection which has to come when you get rejected. I was a little hurt; it hurts to propose to a girl and have her tell you that she doesn't love you.

Pardon me—that she isn't in love with you. There is, as Sara pointed out, a tangible difference.

"Mark?"

I looked at her.

"I told you there were two reasons I wouldn't marry you. That was the first one. Would you like to hear the other or do you want me to pack my suitcase and get the hell out of your life?"

"Of course I want to hear it," I said. "And quit the talk about packing your suitcase, silly."

Her face relaxed into a smile. Then she grew serious again and began talking.

"The second reason is simple," she said. "It's similar to the first one."

"Go ahead."

"You aren't in love with me, Mark."

I almost fell off the desk again. Then I opened my mouth to protest but she was talking again before I could get a word out.

"You aren't," she said. "If you think about it for awhile I think you'll realize that what I'm saying is true. You want to be in love, Mark. You got a promotion last night and you've got both feet on the ground now and you're thinking about getting married. You want a wife, Mark, but you don't want me. I'm just someone who happens to be handy."

"You're wrong."

"I don't think so. Oh, I don't mean to make you sound like an idiot or a guy hell bent for marriage, but I think you'll agree that you thought of getting married before you thought of getting married to me, specifically. Isn't that right?"

I didn't say anything. But I had to admit to myself that she was right. I'd had the whole thing planned before I figured out who the wife would be.

"Look," I said, "I love you."

"Of course you do."

"Then—"

"But you're not in love with me. Are you?"

I thought for a long minute.

"No," I said at length. "No, I guess I'm not."

And I wasn't. I could have married her, could have married her and had children with her and lived all my life with her, and I could have been happy doing it.

But she was right.

I wasn't in love with her.

"Mark?"

"Go ahead."

"I still . . . want to see you. I still want to be with you if and when you want me. This doesn't mean that we have to avoid each other, you know."

"I know."

I also knew that things couldn't ever be quite the same again, not after this morning. We could still see each other and still make love, but there would be always something extra between us, a little barrier set up inhibiting the type of full-blooded relationship we had enjoyed.

"I love you," she said again. "At least as much as you love me. And we're fairly remarkable in bed together, aren't we?"

"We're wonderful together."

"We can still . . . make love. If you want to."

I walked over beside her. I kissed her on the cheek, and I didn't care if every mail clerk in Matterhorn Press was watching us. I felt very much like kissing her just then.

"Have you ever been in love, Mark?"

I shrugged.

"Ever?"

I told her about Elaine. I had never told her before but now I gave her the whole story from start to finish. And as I did this I realized that I hadn't told her about Elaine for a damned good reason, even if I didn't know the reason at the time.

I was still in love with Elaine.

She asked me that when I was done, and I told her that I guessed I probably was. Talking about it, thinking about it, I began to learn a few things about myself. The love I still had for Elaine had a lot to do both with my attitude toward Sara and my performance on the job.

Quite a bit to do with both those things.

When I was all done the coffee break had turned into a free morning. I went back to my own desk and picked up a cold cup of coffee and dropped it into the wastebasket. The cruller followed it.

"Mark—"

I looked at her.

"I suppose I should just keep my mouth shut," she said. "But you're in love with this girl. And you're letting it all go to hell."

"Am I?"

She nodded. "I don't want to tell you how to run your life, Mark. And I'm certainly not going to try telling you what to do with Elaine. But you have to see her. You owe her that much, and you owe it to yourself."

"Why?"

"Because the two of you are in love."

"So?"

"That means something," she told me. "It means a good deal. There are a lot of factors that become less important when two people are in love. Maybe the obstacles in this case are too big, but you ought to see her anyway. You can't try to run away from something like this."

Run away? Was that what I had been doing? That was a hell of a note.

"See her," she said. "It's something you have to do sooner or later, and the sooner the better. If nothing else, it's the only way you'll ever get her out of your system. I've known about her for a long time, Mark."

"How the—"

"I haven't known about *her*, not specifically. But it wasn't hard to tell that there was someone you were trying to forget. Mark, do you realize you never told me you loved me before today?"

"I did, though. It just never seemed necessary to tell you."

"That's just it. It didn't seem necessary because it wasn't necessary, and it wasn't necessary because you were still in love with Elaine, consciously or unconsciously, and you were resisting anything else that might get in the way of that love."

I nodded. I still wasn't sure how much of what she said was true, but it made sense whether it was all true or just an educated guess.

"See her," she told me once again.

"Maybe."

"No maybes. You have to."

•   •   •

I didn't see Elaine, not with the million and one things I had to do. Not with the thinking I had to get out of the way first.

We were busy as wingless bees that week and the next. First of all there was the usual quota of work which had to be done before anything else. I had to rush it, but it wasn't as unbearable as it might have been simply because it was something I wouldn't be doing for the rest of my life. Now that I was set to be something other than traffic manager, managing traffic wasn't nearly as objectionable as it had been when it looked like a lifetime occupation.

Then there was the problem of breaking in a new man. I wanted to make sure whatever joker replaced me had enough of a head on his shoulders so that he could handle the job properly. All we needed was another Les Swift and Matterhorn would be on the ropes and gasping for air in a matter of months. There was a quiet flood of applicants which both Marty and I had to interview, unless they were obvious dolts in which case Marty got rid of them himself. We narrowed the field down and finally decided together to give the job to a young fellow named Don Marshall. Like me he didn't have any experience, but he had a better brain than any of the others and a lot smoother personality. There were two things Marty and I both believed in—hiring men you like and picking personnel on the basis of intelligence. Not IQ—that's meaningless. Brains, moxie, savvy, common sense—call it what you want.

Then, once we settled on Marshall, the fun began. I had to

show him the ropes. There were so damned many ropes and so many other things I had to do that it got a little hectic now and then, but Sara was a help and he learned quick. One way or another we got through it.

I was spending more and more time to myself those days. I saw Sara from time to time and spent a night or two with her now and then, but something was different between us. It wasn't the same and we could sense it. We were still good together, but the scene in my office had killed something that we had previously possessed. Maybe the scene did no more than draw away a curtain that had been hiding reality from us, but in any case we couldn't get back to the stage we had been at before.

It was a shame, in a way. It's very rare for two people to be perfect together. It's even rarer for those two people to love each other.

If we had been *in love*—and remember that this terminology is Sara's and not mine, because only the feminine mind is capable of making such a precise distinction and lousing it up semantically—if we had been in love, everything would have been quite ideal. But we weren't, and now we were finding this fact a limiting factor.

Maybe this was a good development; at least it gave me a lot of time to myself at a point where I sure as hell needed time to myself. I went back to McSwiney's for some casual drinking a few times, getting thoroughly fried once but just having a few and listening to the whiskey tenor the rest of the time. I had lunch at the Blue Boar by myself one afternoon and got mildly sentimental over the second martini remembering the first lunch date with Sara. But then the sauerbraten arrived and all was well again.

You see, I wasn't the rejected lover, not really. And there was nothing to feel particularly glum about, and glumness wasn't really the state I was in. I get depressed with relative ease, but this singular kind of blueness wasn't true depression.

It was more a kind of . . . well, call it loneliness for lack of a better term. The hotel room was getting me down, the dinners by myself were getting me down, and I still wanted a wife and kids as much as I did when I proposed to Sara.

I didn't want Sara now. I recognized what was wrong with that plan.

I wanted Elaine.

Whatever existed between us, whatever we had or didn't have, whatever love we held or didn't hold for each other, we had to meet again. Otherwise I never would find out whether I was coming or going, would never be free to fall in love with anybody else, would go on chasing shadows and calling them Elaine.

I didn't know just where to start. Dropping in on her might be unpleasant, calling her would certainly be a strain. The telephone is a fine invention but its uses are seriously limited in cases of this sort. I had to get in touch with her but it was hard to know where to begin.

The answer seemed obvious when it came to me. Every week I mailed her a check in a blank envelope, with no note enclosed and no return address on the envelope.

So one Friday I wrote her. Just a short note, almost an impersonal note. I wrote it on Matterhorn stationery, the new personal stock that said *Mark Taggert—General Manager* in the upper left-hand corner.

The note went something like this:

Dear Elaine:

I've thought about you a lot since I last saw you. I've been doing a great deal of thinking about a great many things.

If you want to get in touch with me, call me at the office.

Mark

I almost signed it *Love, Mark* but changed my mind at the last minute. I wanted to make it as impersonal and open as possible, in order to give her the fullest opportunity to chuck it in the wastebasket and forget it if she was so inclined. I didn't want to push her into anything, and certainly not into a resumption of the affair with me. That wouldn't do either of us a hell of a lot of good, and it might louse us both up in due course.

I folded the letter, wrapped up the check in it, and mailed it in a Matterhorn envelope. Then I went back to the room, settled my hotel bill for the coming week, had a quick and relatively tasteless dinner, and killed a few hours listening to jazz at the Five Spot, a top modern club downtown on Cooper Square. Randy Weston was on piano with a group of hard bop sidemen and the night went by very pleasantly. I almost forgot about Elaine there for awhile.

Then a cab back to the hotel. Then my clothes to the closet and myself to bed.

I dreamed about her.

CHAPTER 12

The weekend was pretty horrible.

I knocked around by myself Saturday. After lunch I wandered down to Times Square and prowled around from bookstore to movie house to hot dog stand. I went to the flea circus and watched the fleas perform—which, if you have never seen it before, is something of a spectacle. There are all these fleas, you see, and you have to look at them through a magnifying glass. The little beggars do tricks like hauling miniature carts fifty times their own weight and like that.

There was this dame standing next to me watching them, a sort of frizzled, painted, busty and hippy wench who looked like a whore on her monthly vacation. She was standing right next to me with her tail bumping me in the hip intermittently, and absently she was scratching that tail of hers with the brightly painted fingernails of her right hand.

Well, a guy can take so much. Here's this battered little bim scratching herself, and here are all these fleas, and before too long a guy's mind starts making unpleasant associations. In a few more minutes I felt a little itchy and flea bitten myself, and it was time to bid a fond adieu to the flea circus and find another scene.

I wandered some more. I listened to an unintelligible sidewalk preacher trying to lead the world back to the ways of righteousness—and Times Square was obviously the place to start, even if the chances of success were a lot slimmer than they might have been in Nowhere, Utah. This guy had less chance than usual for the simple reason that it was totally impossible to understand what in the world he was talking about. He mumbled and ranted and stormed, and every once in awhile I caught a word or two, but the bulk of his spiel went out the window.

This didn't bother the mob of chowderheads who stood around listening to him. That's one of the fascinating things about New York—people will watch or listen to virtually anything. One time I saw a horse trample a taxi on Sixth Avenue— yeah, a horse. There are a batch of horse-drawn hansoms that take starlit couples for moonlit rides in Central Park, and this particular hansom was on its merry way to the park when the horse got sick of the whole thing.

The animal was disturbed, highly disturbed, and he reared way up in the air with hooves rampant. He came down on a cab that didn't have a chance to get out of the way, and those rampant hooves romped all over the left fender and wrecked havoc wherever they landed.

All of which served to infuriate the horse, not to mention the poor son of a bitch driving the cab. The horse got so mad he reared again and stoved in the roof of the hack. Then the driver finally got the fool horse under control and pulled him over to the curb, slipping a feed-bag in front of his silly face and stroking his head to pacify him, or whatever you do with a rampant horse.

Then the cabby pulled over, too, and you could see what was going through his mind. There wasn't much chance that anybody had had the foresight to take out ten-and-twenty liability insurance on the horse, especially since nobody but Lloyd's of London would conceive of writing a policy like that.

And how in the world was the guy going to explain what had happened to his company?

"There was this horse," he would say. "Yeah, I was driving down Sixth and this horse . . . like he came and stomped the cab. Yeah, this horse. What do you mean what the hell was I drinking?"

And like that.

Anyway, the point of all this horsefeathers is that there were at least two hundred foolish people crowded around while all this was going on. They stared, they talked, and they otherwise enjoyed themselves. No one tried to do anything to help, no one called a cop—no one did anything but stare like a petrified cow.

So after I got tired of staring at the broken-down preacher like a petrified cow I went over to one of the Times Square book-shops which have a good line of second-hand paperbacks at cut-rate prices. I picked up three or four books, paid the guy at the register, and lugged the books back to my room.

I finished one of the books a little after one in the morning.

I fell asleep.

I slept late Sunday afternoon. I stayed in bed until I couldn't stand it any longer, then got up and took a shower. After I had finished the shower I decided a bath would be a particularly enjoyable way to relax, so I filled the tub up, set a pack of cigarettes next to it and crawled into it with a book in my hand.

The bath turned out to be an exceptionally nice way to avoid Sunday. I just stayed there in the lukewarm water until I had plowed my way through the second book, and then I got out, drained the tub, blotted my waterlogged skin and got dressed.

I was starving by this time so I went out and bought myself a blood-rare steak. With the steak nestled in my stomach along with a big baked potato for companionship, I went back to my hotel room and dived into another paperback novel.

It was one hell of a weekend, let me tell you.

I read myself to sleep again. It took a long time for me to wear myself out, and when the guy at the desk rang me Monday morning my eyes were glued together and my mouth tasted as though some goon had been using it for an ashtray. Or maybe for a spittoon. Cold water took care of my eyes and the toothbrush took care of my mouth and black coffee combined with cigarette took care of the general sogginess of my brain.

I walked to the office. It was good weather—clear and crisp the way autumn in New York is supposed to be, if you believe the songs. This was late for autumn—almost winter, to be exact. The fall rush was gone and the January rush was starting, with college bookstores all over the bloody country ordering their texts for the second semester and bitching like bitches if the books didn't arrive two days after they sent in their orders.

On top of this we were up to our ears in a new promotion campaign, the one I had dreamed up and was almost sorry for already. There were estimates from printers to go over, advertising charts to mull and miscellaneous garbage to ponder in my spare moments. Since I didn't have any spare moments this made things a little bit difficult.

Just to make things even more difficult, it was Monday. Now on Monday there is mail. Lots of mail. Tons of mail. The Saturday mail was waiting for me when I walked in the door, and the mail that represented Sunday and Monday flooded the office early and kept pouring in.

Mail.

Too damned much mail.

Sara was a half hour late, which didn't help things. I had to get started by myself, and I was on edge enough expecting a phone call from Elaine. She would get my letter that morning, and she might call any minute.

Then again, she might not call at all.

Which is what had me on edge.

Hell, what would I say to her if she did call? *Let's make a little music in your bed*—that would be nice. Or maybe *I've had a change of heart; let me come over so you can buy me another meal.*

Yeah.

What with all the work and all the mail and the constant round of interruptions that seemed to accompany the job of general manager, things went not too smoothly at all. What with all the tension within me over the possibly-approaching phone call from Elaine, things went very roughly to say the least.

Sara and I sent out for lunch. This wasn't unusual—at least it was fairly common for me to phone down to the delicatessen for a sandwich and a cup of coffee during my lunch hour. But Sara almost always went out for lunch.

This time I didn't have the time to spare. She had to eat in also, and that's an indication of how damnably busy we were.

Lunch was corned beef on rye, a side of well done French fries and a big sour dill pickle with a bottle of cream soda to wash it all down. After lunch we went at it again, belching across the room at each other from the pickles and sandwiches and cream soda.

We weren't done by five.

And Elaine hadn't called.

Staying late didn't bother me nearly so much as the lack of a call from Elaine did. Sara and I just kept right on going while the rest of the floor emptied itself, waving away the woman who wanted to mop the floor and empty the wastebasket and working on into the night. The sky darkened gradually, the process speeding up when the lights went out one after another in the building across the street. I ordered dinner from the deli—lox and cream cheese this time, with the omnipresent pickle and with coffee instead of the treacherous cream soda.

Then back to work.

More work.

And more gloom.

By the time we ran out of work I felt like hell. It was time to go but I didn't feel like going any place. I felt like staying in the office and working until I dropped, but there didn't seem to be any more work to do.

For a moment or two I toyed with the idea of dropping in on

Elaine, but it didn't take too long to decide against it. She had to make her move—I had given her an opening, and anything more on my part would be too aggressive.

But waiting can be a pain.

Yeah.

CHAPTER 13

Elaine.

She called the next afternoon just after I had gotten back from lunch. The phone rang and I picked it up, not expecting that it would be her.

"Mark Taggert," I said.

"I'll be home tonight if you want to see me." That was all she said, and before I could say a word the phone clicked in my ear as she hung up the receiver.

I'll be home tonight if you want to see me.

And I wanted to see her.

I looked at my watch—over three hours remained before work would be done for the day. I considered taking the afternoon off, but I dropped the idea. Too much work, and I didn't want to rush things with her anyway. She had said she would be home in the evening; I would go to her, but I would wait until evening.

Work dragged. Work dragged hopelessly, with too much to do and nothing much that was interesting enough to make the time pass in a hurry. In between letters I told Sara about Elaine's call. She wished me luck, but I wasn't quite sure what would be lucky.

I thought five o'clock would never come.

It did, though. It fooled me.

It was the better part of a mile from Matterhorn's offices to Elaine's hotel, and it was a cold and fairly unpleasant evening, but I walked the distance just the same. I wanted time, sparring time, time to go over in my mind by myself the approach I would use. It didn't do much good. I walked over to Park and downtown toward her hotel, barely aware of where I was going with my mind in a fog and my feet approximately half an inch off the ground all the way there. I was confused.

Confused is hardly the word for it. I was hopelessly mixed up. I didn't know where Elaine stood, or even where I stood, for that matter. I tried to figure it out and didn't get anywhere special.

So I gave up figuring. When I got to her hotel I waved half-heartedly to her doorman—who didn't seem to recognize me any more—and mumbled to the elevator operator, whom I didn't recognize myself.

I got off the elevator at her floor and approached her door very slowly. I stood in front of it for a long while before I managed to knock feebly on it. Then I waited an ungodly length of time before she answered the door.

She was the most beautiful woman in the world.

What else can I say? It was all I could think, all I could feel, all I could smell or touch or hear or taste. It was Elaine, and the second I saw her I knew that I loved her at that moment more than I had ever loved her before, more than I had imagined possible.

She reacted the same way. It was plain to see—in her eyes, in the trembling of her shoulders, in the thin red line of her mouth.

She motioned me inside. She didn't speak; I don't think she was able to speak at the moment. She was as nervous as I was, and I was more nervous than I had ever been before in my life. I followed her inside and walked to the couch and sat down.

She closed the door and sat down beside me.

The stage was set. There were two martinis on the little coffee table, a Vivaldi concerto on the hi-fi.

And we were together on the couch.

I looked at her.

Neither of us could speak.

She opened her mouth to say something. The words wouldn't come out, and to help her I reached out one hand and touched her shoulder.

The touch did it. It broke the tension, and the next second she was in my arms, holding me tight, pressing the softness of herself against me.

And crying.

Crying.

For the first time she was crying, crying real tears that streamed down her face onto my suit jacket. And this broke whatever barrier might still have remained between us. It was her concession to me, that crying, and it was the hardest concession for a proud and beautiful woman like Elaine to make.

Everything else, every small obstacle to our happiness, was suddenly petty and unimportant and easily surmountable. Every factor that separated us before dissolved quickly and quietly in the salty stream of her tears. Our love was stronger than ever, stronger than the love of any other man for any other woman.

She cried, and I held her in my arms and stroked the soft skin of the back of her neck with fingers that were trembling for love of her.

No words were spoken; no words were needed. We were too close and too much in love to bother with words. She was still crying when I stood up and carried her in my arms to the bedroom.

She continued to cry while I lay down beside her and took her in my arms.

There were no preliminaries, no kisses or caresses. There was only a pair of bodies in love, two bodies that became one amidst the overwhelming magic of physical and spiritual love, love that overshadowed and overpowered everything, love that left only us, only ourselves wrapped up in the mystery and beauty of two beings in love.

She went on crying throughout it all. She was crying with love, crying with joy, crying with happiness. Her tears flowed freely and wet my face.

Before we were through other drops of salty moisture also wet my face.

They were tears also.

My own.

We loved each other.

We loved each other all that night, and we still love each other, and we will continue to love each other as long as we live.

And love is a very beautiful, wonderful, magical and mystical thing.

A many-splendored thing, as the song says. And the song is right.

We were married a few days after that night. There was a blood test first which we both passed with flying colors, and a three-day waiting period which was sheer agony, and a wedding ceremony performed by a Justice of the Peace with two unknowns for witnesses.

That was the way we wanted it.

And there was a honeymoon, with a three-week vacation graciously provided by Marty and a cruise to the West Indies, with a shipboard cabin that we filled with love and a hotel room in Jamaica that we nearly set on fire when I let a cigarette burn itself out in an ashtray because I was too busy with other things at the time.

We loved each other.

At the end of the three weeks our boat was back in New York and I returned to my job at Matterhorn. Theoretically the honeymoon was over, but in fact it went on.

It is going on to this day.

It will go on forever.

Because we love each other.

Love is a very strange thing. It was hard, very hard, inconceivably hard after that one night for us to believe that her money had kept us apart.

I couldn't understand how I had left her because I was unwilling to help her spend her money.

She couldn't understand how she could have refused to live on my salary.

We couldn't understand how on earth we had managed to become separated.

But we agreed on one thing—the separation was good, even necessary. If it did nothing else, it proved to both of us how much we needed each other. It gave us time to live and time to grow so that we were both able to love each other better after the separation had ended.

The separation from Elaine coupled with the love for Elaine forced me to work much harder than I might have worked otherwise. I had to prove to myself that I could make the grade on my own—and I did.

I still work at Matterhorn, of course. I'm general manager there now, and in a few years I'll probably be a full partner. Marty doesn't have any kids and his wife died several years ago—I'm practically a son to him.

He's practically a father to me, for that matter. And to Elaine. He's over to the house for dinner one or two nights a week nowadays, and he's pushing us to name the first boy Martin.

Yeah, our house. The Park Avenue hotel was convenient and comfortable and all, but we wanted something more permanent, something that went better with marriage and love and permanence. We have a big and beautiful home now, a huge stone house in Pound Ridge in Upper Westchester County. The place used to be a mansion when the Dutch patroons controlled this part of the state, and the Dutch had the right idea when it came to building houses. Big, massive, with high ceilings and thick walls and plenty of space. We had to do a lot of remodeling but it was worth it.

There's one room just for music, with a flawless hi-fi system and a cabinet filled with the records we both like. There's another room just for books, with three walls lined with floor-to-ceiling bookshelves and heavy wine-red leather chairs that are perfect for sitting in. The grounds are spacious and there are trees in the backyard.

It's a good place for people.

A good place for kids, too.

Yeah, kids. The first one's on the way now. We didn't want to waste any time; we figured we'd wasted enough time as it was.

We've decided to take a trip to Europe—we can fit in a Grand Tour of our own before the kid's big enough to show too much. And prenatal influence just might mean something, in which case it can't hurt for the kid to absorb a little culture.

Nor, for that matter, can it hurt for the kid's old man to absorb a little culture. I've never been to Europe and I'm looking forward to it. Elaine's been across several times but she's looking forward to it as much as I am, if not more. She says it'll be different seeing the same places with me.

Let me tell you what I've got now. I've got more money than I can possibly spend. I've got a good home and a good job and a good boss. I'm married to the most beautiful, wonderful woman in the world.

I happen to love her.

She happens to love me.

I'm a very happy guy, you see. I haven't taken a survey but I wouldn't be a bit surprised if I'm the happiest guy going.

My wife's income is more than ten times as high as mine is.

Perhaps you think this makes me a gigolo. Perhaps you happen to feel that this little fact will keep me from respecting myself. Perhaps you don't think I have any right to be the happiest guy going.

Is that what you think? If it is, I have some advice for you. You can take it or leave it, but I'd prefer it if you'd take it. It would make me very happy, even happier than I already am, if you would heed the following message. It's simple advice, just three little words:

Go to hell.

My Newsletter: I get out an email newsletter at unpredictable intervals, but rarely more often than every other week. I'll be happy to add you to the distribution list. A blank email to lawbloc@gmail.com with "newsletter" in the subject line will get you on the list, and a click of the "Unsubscribe" link will get you off it, should you ultimately decide you're happier without it.

Lawrence Block has been writing award-winning mystery and suspense fiction for half a century. You can read his thoughts about crime fiction and crime writers in *The Crime of Our Lives*, where this MWA Grand Master tells it straight. His most recent novels are *The Girl With the Deep Blue Eyes*; *The Burglar Who Counted the Spoons*, featuring Bernie Rhodenbarr; *Hit Me,* featuring Keller; and *A Drop of the Hard Stuff,* featuring Matthew Scudder, played by Liam Neeson in the film *A Walk Among the Tombstones.* Several of his other books have been filmed, although not terribly well. He's well known for his books for writers, including the classic *Telling Lies for Fun &f Profit,* and *The Liar's Bible.* In addition to prose works, he has written episodic television (*Tilt!*) and the Wong Kar-wai film, *My Blueberry Nights.* He is a modest and humble fellow, although you would never guess as much from this biographical note.

Email: lawbloc@gmail.com
Twitter: @LawrenceBlock
Facebook: lawrence.block
Website: lawrenceblock.com

Printed in the USA
CPSIA information can be obtained
at www.ICGtesting.com
LVHW021311050724
784683LV00035B/752